ORC HAI!

THOMAS FULTON

One Printers Way
Altona, MB R0G 0B0
Canada www.friesenpress.com

Copyright © 2025 by Thomas Fulton
First Edition — 2025

All rights reserved.

No part of this publication may be reproduced in any form, or by any means, electronic or mechanical, including photocopying, recording, or any information browsing, storage, or retrieval system, without permission in writing from FriesenPress.

Cover illustration by Patricia Grace Claro
Map illustration by Eric Hotz

ISBN
978-1-03-834737-4 (Hardcover)
978-1-03-834736-7 (Paperback)
978-1-03-834738-1 (eBook)

1. Fiction, Fantasy, Cozy

Distributed to the trade by The Ingram Book Company

ORC HAI!

THOMAS FULTON

Map

N ↑

- Tharan-Dum
- Majestic Mtns
- Ered Chimera Mts
- Chimera
- Foot Hills
- Anvil
- The Great North-South Road
- O'Roarke's Station
- LAKE
- Howling Hills
- HAGHILL
- Cornerbrook
- HOT & DRY
- SWARTH LAND PLAINS
- HOT & DRY
- COUNCIL LAKE
- Alhambra
- EDRADOUR
- WEST MARSHES

BOOK 1

Prologue

"Orc!" A cry that evokes fear and revulsion in all that hear it.

Orcs are truly a grotesque creature and a thoroughly degenerate species, possessing few, if any, redeeming qualities. They are squat and broad built humanoids with bowed legs, standing five feet six to six feet in height. Their skin varies from a sickening green to gray and is often covered with short, bristly brown or black hair. Beady black eyes, canine-like ears with large flat noses above a jutting jaw and short lower tusk gave them a pig-like look.

They are loud, unruly and quarrelsome, exhibiting no discipline unless it is beaten into them. Given the opportunity, they will fight each other as readily as an enemy.

Above all, their most serious drawback is their aversion to sunlight. Even so, their numbers continue to rise and, if this wasn't bad enough, they are being crossbred by all manner of evil warlord and sorcerer in hopes of creating a superior species. Thus, the proliferation of the subspecies half-orc.

As you might expect, the variations in this species, is quite dramatic. The most sought-after half-orc species are six to six and a half feet tall, with gray or green skin and sparsely covered by that same coarse brown to black hair.

In many ways, they are similar in **appearance** to orc, but possess brown or black eyes. There primary advantages over orcs are their size, strength and intelligence (although this last one is minimal) and that they have no aversion to sunlight.

In the northern frontier settlement of Chimera, one such warlord, an evil cleric by the name of Kemac and his sorceress companion, Helene, were busy breeding an army by using human captives to breed half-orcs—both male and female—as part of their sick plan to build an empire.

These offspring half-orc were sorted into two groups. The suitable stock joined Kemac's burgeoning army, while females and those deemed too small or scrawny were rejected and marked either for combat practice or slaves.

The real irony was that Kemac had succeeded in his attempt to breed a superior subspecies of half-orc, only he did not recognize it as he was too fixated on size.

That success was Freya and her sisters: Fina, Scara, Uta, Pohla and Tauna. The sisters stood no taller than an average orc and, being female, they were immediately rejected and used as slaves, their masters believing females would never be robust enough for combat.

Freya and her sisters were not true sisters for only Freya and Fina were siblings. The title of sisters referred to them being sisters in misery.

Freya was different from her dark brown hair and eyes, light green-brown complexion to her small, upturned nose. Her features were sharply defined and angular, making her appear more human than orc. But what truly made her different was her intelligence, intuition and reflexes.

1

The settlement of Chimera was located in the foothills of the Ered Chimera Mountains and was comprised of a four-story citadel and a small settlement. It was home to a few hundred men, orc and half-orc, whose numbers were on the rise.

The Citadel was a rectangular stone tower thirty feet long by forty feet wide and surrounded by a windowless two-story stone blockhouse, topped with parapets. Evenly spaced along the second floor of the blockhouse were arrow ports for bow or crossbows to be fired from, while up on the parapets, a ballista was mounted at each corner. For added defense, a pair of heavy, ballista, were mounted on top of the citadel and designed to cover all areas of the settlement.

The masters of Chimera were the evil cleric Kemac and sorceress Helene, who employed sixty or so well-armed men-at-arms, all of whom resided in the relative luxury of the citadel and surrounding blockhouse. These men at arms were well trained, well fed and generally cruel.

The settlement itself (to use the term loosely) was comprised of a series of compounds, each surrounded by a wooden palisade. Beyond that was an outer stockade.

This stockade was a semi-circular wooden wall built of vertically placed tree trunks, sharpened at both ends and then embedded into the ground. They were then lashed tightly together to form a solid wall. Each end of the stockade wall butted up against the cliffs behind.

The stockade employed a raised catwalk to allow the defenders the ability to fight off any attacker from behind its protection.

Scattered around the interior of the stockade and quartered in separate wooden pen-like compounds were human, orc and half-orc captives. These compounds were deliberately built to segregate the different groups from each other, thereby keeping them from indiscriminately mixing or harming one another. This was especially true between the orc and half-orc who hated one another.

If you think that this configuration resembles breeding pens, you would be correct in that hypothesis. This was where Kemac and Helene bred an army to dominate the frontier.

Nearest to the stockade was a squalid hovel loosely referred to as the Village. The Village itself was home to an assortment of shops and amenities catering to the guard's needs.

Herds of cattle grazed in the foothills while small tracts of land were worked by slave labor. These activities provided much needed food and nearly as importantly the illusion of normalcy.

The land this far north was not overly fertile, requiring much more work to produce crops. The shorter growing season did not help, making hunting and raiding essential to supplement the shortfall.

These activities were carefully selected by Kemac as to not draw unwanted attention towards Chimera and the Ered Chimera mountains until he was ready to deal with his nosy and troublesome neighbors.

Tonight, Freya and her sisters, Fina, Tauna, Scara and Pohla, tended one of their own, Uta. They called themselves sisters because they considered themselves sisters in misery. In fact, only Freya and Fina shared the same mother.

Returning to their shelter late one evening and exhausted from a hard day's work, Uta was caught unaware by a group of drunken human guardsmen. She was callously beaten and raped, then, once they were bored with her, they tossed her into the orc compound just for the fun of it.

And fun Uta became: she was brutally abused, then tossed and kicked around like the ball in some sick game of polo until she was barely alive or recognizable.

This only stopped when she quit moving or moaning, for she was no longer fun and they tossed her like refuse from their compound, enabling Fina and Tauna to retrieve her broken, near lifeless body.

Uta had looked so much like Scara, they could have been twins: from her long black hair and brown-black eyes to her upturned nose, prominent jaw and teeth.

A fine short, dark hair covered portions of her olive brown skin. At best her features could be described as severe and, like all her sisters, she stood just over five feet tall.

Fina and Tauna carried Uta back to the small shelter they all shared in the slave compound. Her injuries were too many and too serious for anything they could do. All they could do was make her comfortable until she died, very slowly and painfully.

Perhaps a healing potion or a healing spell might have saved her, but such luxury was not wasted on slaves.

It was as Uta gasped her last breath that Freya came to a decision. No more of her sisters would suffer the same fate as Uta. She would find a way for them to escape.

This was radical thinking for any slave let alone a half-breed like Freya, but she possessed much of her mother and, through a quirk of breeding, was highly intuitive and intelligent.

The key to survival in Chimera was to remain unnoticed and always be aware of your surroundings. That is what got Uta: she failed to notice the guards until it was too late.

They had all learned early to disguise themselves to look less desirable. Freya, on a good day or in poor light, could pass for a pure-blooded human. Only Pohla possessed nearly all her birth mother's physical traits. She could easily be described as petite and pretty, with long light brown hair and brilliant green-brown eyes. Her fine features and fair complexion would have made her a desirable prey for the men of Chimera, so she had been pronounced dead at birth. From then on, Pohla remained disguised and hidden.

"Enough is enough!" Freya began. "We will not suffer the same fate as Uta."

"What can we do? It is our fate." Scara muttered despondently.

"Here we are and here we will die!" Tauna wailed.

ORC HAI!

Tauna had a medium build with dark black hair and dark brown eyes, a pale olive complexion, a small flat nose and angular lips giving her a sharp look.

"Yes," Fina agreed, "here we are and here we will surely die. If not tomorrow then the day after."

"That may be true if we stay here but I—we will not be staying here!" Freya addressed them passionately to convince her sisters as she was beginning to form a plan.

"Not here? Where would we go Freya?" Pohla spoke for the first time since the recovery of Uta.

"Anywhere would be better than here! There is a whole world out there. But first we will need to collect supplies. For now, we must bury Uta. Then we will discuss how to collect supplies and equipment."

"What sort of supplies and where will we get them?" Her sisters asked in near unison.

"We will steal them," Freya ordered. "We will need traveling clothes, food, tools and, most importantly, armor and weapons to defend ourselves." Freya detailed her plan as quickly as it formed in her head.

"But what if we are caught? They will not hesitate to—" Tauna began nervously.

"Then we will join Uta sooner rather than later. But we will not be caught. They pay us little attention. We will just have to blend in better so they will notice us even less!" Freya tolerated no further discussion of failure.

There was a brief pause while the others considered her words, then Tauna spoke up. "Traveling clothes should not be a problem. I can get animal hides and a small amount of cloth. I can make the clothes."

"Travel rations, I can get travel rations. Only a few each time a raid goes out." Fina volunteered.

Travel rations at Chimera were rather basic. Well, that was being generous. They consisted of hard biscuits, dried meat of some kind and watered down mead. There were no fruits or vegetables as these were not popular with either the orc or half-orc but these were fine for Freya and her sisters whose diets were a little better.

Freya smiled: it looked like she had gotten her sisters to buy into her idea and now the enthusiasm began to build.

"Weapons and armor will be more difficult," Scara mused. "Short swords and bows or possible light crossbows may be easiest. Our heroic warriors are always misplacing, losing or breaking them." her voice dripped with loathing.

"Now, armor—that will be really tricky for it needs to be fitted to the wearer. Hardened leather would be easiest but metal armor would be better; only I cannot see how we will be able to steal any of that." Scara finished.

"Now," Freya began, "I want all of you to promise that, from now on, you will never work alone, always work in twos or threes so you can look out for each other. This way, none of us should suffer the same fate as Uta."

They looked from one to another, considering this. Never before had they considered making a concerted effort to stick together. After all, they were slaves and did what they were told. Perhaps their odd action might be noticed.

In reality, no one paid much attention or cared about what a slave might be doing unless a task was not accomplished. Unfortunately, Uta had just been tired and in the wrong place at the wrong time. For, inside the stockade, brutality was rampant and random.

"Good! Then it is decided. We know what we need to do. Work only in two, or threes. Once we collect all we need, we will leave," Freya reiterated the plan. She then paused to ensure they all understood before continuing. "Now we must bury our sister."

Normally, orc or even half-orc had little regard for the dead beyond stripping them of any valuables and desecrating the bodies. What this small group proposed to do made them quite different.

It was something they had picked up from the many human slaves they had been in contact with and a radical departure in attitude clearly separating them from their half-bred cousins.

It was twilight when the five of them carefully lifted Uta's body and carried it unseen to a secret place just inside the stockade wall, near the cliffs. The stockade was not designed to keep its residents inside. That was the job of the individual compounds. Their masters believed that there was no place to run so the wooden stockade wall was there to keep others out.

Unobserved, they laid Uta to rest, burying her meager belongings with her. They could not dig a deep hole so they placed large stones atop her grave to ensure her body remained undisturbed by animals. Then left a small nondescript gravestone.

In lieu of a prayer, for none were spiritual, Freya spoke briefly. "We wish you could still be with us, Uta, but you have inspired us. Rest peacefully; we will not forget you." The others repeated rest peacefully; we will not forget you.

This was the closest thing to a prayer Freya and her sisters knew. Sad but heartened and with a new sense of purpose, they returned to their shelter in the slave compound.

2

Within a few days, Freya, Fina and Tauna had obtained a large quantity of leather and fur. Tauna, who was by far the best and fastest seamstress of the group, was set to work fashioning traveling clothes.

The biggest surprise of the next few days came from the quiet and shy Pohla. She had made a real find by being able to salvage a complete set of hardened leather armor from a troublesome and now dead orc.

He had been killed and then thrown to the hounds. The hounds had treated his body like a new toy and tore him apart. Somehow, his armor remained pretty much intact.

Even soiled with blood, it was an amazing find and, although too large to fit any of them, it demonstrated how the armor was fashioned and could be used as a pattern.

However happy Freya was about the armor, she was shocked that Pohla had taken such a risk retrieving it. "This is wonderful, Pohla, but those hounds could have easily made a lunch of you. Please! You must be more careful!"

"Sorry, Freya."

As they all examined the armor, Pohla tried to explain to a distracted Freya how she was on good terms with the hounds.

Over the next few days, two large raiding parties departed, leaving the settlement comparatively quiet. This allowed Freya and her sisters more, free time to work on clothing and gather needed supplies.

They also realized that working in pairs made their chores easier so they were able to finish these tasks faster, thereby leaving them more free time. Another positive of these raids was that it allowed Fina to collect a tidy supply of travel rations.

This slower more leisurely pace came to an abrupt end when a trade caravan returned, throwing the whole settlement into a frenzy of activity. The caravan was carrying vast quantities of supplies: the old ones, even the odd weapon, needed to be tossed out to make room for the influx of all the new supplies. It was to prove a good time to pilfer, as Scara put it.

"Look!" she crowed in triumph as she extracted a small bolt of fine linen out from a bundle of rags.

Fina and Tauna looked up expectantly but were unimpressed. Even Freya could not understand Scara's excitement. Sure, the bolt of linen was needed but surely nothing to get that excited about; or so Freya thought, until Scara withdrew an undamaged short sword from inside the bolt of linen. Scara beamed with pride as everyone else's jaws dropped.

"Some fool threw it out!" She exclaimed, dancing with glee. "I was rummaging through a pile of old leather and found it. All I had to do was find something to hide it in."

ORC HAI!

"And no one has missed it?" Freya asked as she studied the sword. As their leader, Freya tended to fuss over details the others ignored.

"It has been there all day and no one has asked about it. I only just went back for it. As you say, I feared such a fine weapon would be noticed missing!" Scara explained.

"It appears our luck is changing!" Freya ventured as she scanned the growing pile of supplies (clothes, rope, bedrolls, cooking gear). As if seeing their stash for the first time, Freya experienced a shock at the quantity.

"We must find someplace else to store this stuff. Somewhere safe, preferably outside the stockade and easy for us to retrieve."

"I know a place." Pohla piped up; only no one heard her over Scara.

"There is more, I could not carry it all. There are pieces of hardened leather, some as big as this." Scara used her hands to demonstrate the size.

"That is excellent, Scara," Freya complimented her. "Wait," Freya felt she had missed something—wait, Pohla had spoken. "Pohla, what did you say?"

"I know a place." Pohla asserted again.

"You do?"

"Yes! A secret place well outside the stockade. I found it when I was out with the hounds," she stopped, seeing their shocked expressions.

Her sisters looked at her horrified. Everyone knew the hounds were to be feared.

"What?" Pohla asked startled. "Odred lets me take the boys out to hunt."

Apparently, none of them knew about her bond with the hounds—well, at least two in particular—or her ability to handle them. Not so surprising considering Pohla seldom spoke and when she did, it was always very softly. There was a group pause while the others tried to digest that bit of startling news.

"This is all good—yes—very good!" Freya spoke slowly while she considered this rather startling bit of information and its possible ramifications.

"Scara, you, Fina and Tauna go collect that leather. I will go with Pohla and have a look at this secret place to see if it is acceptable." Freya finished then rose to signify everyone should depart to fulfill their appointed tasks.

It was already late in the evening and the sun was casting long shadows. With darkness falling, they slipped silently, one after another, out of their shelter. Curiously enough, no one particularly cared what slaves did here in Chimera as long as everything got done, but it was still best if you remained inconspicuous.

Unseen by the guards, Pohla led Freya from their shelter out and around the hound's pen. The hounds were huge beasts, taller than Great Danes but built like big, hairy bears.

A pair of the huge brutes must have gotten her scent and suddenly came bounding over, sticking their huge, hairy bulldog-like heads through the wooden fence posts. Freya's heart nearly stopped, for she thought the jig was up. Then, to her horror, Pohla reached out and began stroking their heads.

"Brutus, Rocky, good boys!" She spoke to them like children as she fussed over the two big heads.

ORC HAI!

Freya knew if she had tried that, these same brutes would have ripped her arms off. Pohla had no such trouble; the pair lapped up her attention.

"No! No walk now. Be good boys now and go home!" she coaxed them. Brutus and Rocky paused, obviously torn between obeying and a desire for more attention. "Go!" Pohla commanded firmly, her tone brokering no disobedience.

Obedience won out and they turned to depart the way they had come, with many a backward glance hoping she would call them back.

Freya looked at Pohla with awe. "I know you told us but until I saw it with my own eyes I would not have believed it. It is not that I did not believe you but it is just so incredible," Freya paused still trying to grasp what she had just seen. "You are very good with them. How long have you been working with them?"

"Since they were pups. I told you that Odred their handler lets me take the boys out." Pohla seemed puzzled and hurt that none of her sisters, especially Freya, seemed to know this.

"Well," Freya paused in sudden thought. What had she supposed Pohla was doing? Frankly, now that Freya thought about it, she had to admit that she knew so little about Pohla. She had always been the shy and quiet one.

They had all worked so hard when she was young to hide her from the men and obviously all that hard work had worked too well.

"Honestly, Pohla, I am ashamed to admit I assumed you had found a quiet place to hide to avoid some extra duties." Extra duty for a female usually meant warming the bed of some drunk. "We tried so hard to make you invisible. I guess it worked too well. I am sorry."

"It is okay Freya!" Pohla responded wiping away a tear.

"No, it is not and for that I am truly sorry, Pohla." Freya reached out and pulled Pohla to her. "I will try not to make that mistake again. Please forgive me!" Freya gave her another hug.

"I understand, Freya," There was a brief pause as she wiped her eyes. "We should get moving."

The stockade wall loomed ahead, and both knew silence was needed as they neared it. The wall's timbers were large and, for the most part, tightly lashed together except where the wall neared the cliff.

It was here that the occasional gap showed. Not large gaps but, perhaps with a little bit of work, they could be made passable for someone small. The real trick was to conceal it so it would not be noticed and the alarm sounded.

Kemac and Helene rarely left the citadel and would never be caught wandering the compound. However, the captain of the guard took his job very seriously. He regularly inspected the stockade and troops.

Pohla approached what looked like a solid stretch of wall. Stopping, she knelt by a knotted pole then, reaching down, she removed what looked to be a much larger rock than it truly was. Firmly gripping the pole with both hands, she skillfully twisted it to reveal a gap just wide enough to pass through. Well, wide enough if you were small like they were. With a quick look around and a glance through the gap, both women slipped through.

ORC HAI!

Once on the other side, Pohla twisted the timber pole back into place, concealing the gap. In the gathering darkness, the spot would be near impossible to see unless you knew where to look.

Pohla wasted no time in leading Freya away from the stockade, skirting the hillside, using the varying levels of the ground along with the limited foliage to avoid detection. The guards manning the stockade would see nothing for, unlike Freya and Pohla, they did not have excellent night vision: another positive bi-product of their breeding.

Pohla disappeared around a rocky outcrop as Freya paused to look back at the way they had come. She had never seen Chimera from the outside before and when she turned back to follow, Pohla was nowhere to be seen.

Freya froze as a moment of panic gripped her. She began to look around desperately. Where was Pohla? Where had she gotten too? She was about to call out but immediately stopped herself. Out here, her voice would carry too far. Then, just as suddenly, Pohla was back beside her.

"Pohla, you nearly scared the life out of me! Where did you go?" Freya asked in a hushed tone.

"Sorry! I thought you were right behind me." Pohla apologized in a whisper.

"I was. I only paused to look back for a few seconds and when I turned around, you were gone. Where did you go?" Freya was still rattled and spoke more harshly than she intended.

"Sorry! I thought you were right behind me. So, when I turned around and you did not follow me in, I came back out to look for you. Come! It is just over here." Pohla kept apologizing, feeling she had let Freya down.

Freya realized her mistake and, again, she had wrongfully upset Pohla. "Now it is I who must again apologize to you, Pohla. You have done nothing wrong. I should have been paying more attention. So where is this secret place of yours?" Freya looked past Pohla and saw nothing.

"Here!" Pohla pulled back some bushes and slipped behind them.

Freya was a little dubious but followed only to find a small fissure in the rock behind the bushes. The fissure looked barely large enough to squeeze through but obviously Pohla had slipped through, so Freya gave it a go and was surprised to find the fissure was much wider than it first appeared.

The fissure entrance itself was only a couple of feet thick before it opened into a roughly circular cave, approximately forty feet wide by fifteen feet high—and this was only the beginning. Beyond the initial cave, a cavern extended far back, out of sight.

Even with her excellent night vision, Freya could see only a small portion of the cave they had entered. She could make out Pohla just ahead of her then heard a sharp crack followed almost immediately by the flash of a tiny spark from Pohla's fire-starting kit. All at once, a small oil lamp sputtered to life. Freya's night-vision was fine but not nearly as good as a pure-bred orc or goblin, so a little illumination was helpful and welcome.

The cave came into crisp focus and it was obvious to her that it was naturally formed; the stone floor was covered with

ORC HAI!

fine sand, which tended to settle in the low spots, leveling the floor somewhat.

Freya looked around in wonder. "It is perfect!" she exclaimed. "However, did you find this place, Pohla?"

Pohla beamed with pride, pleased and happy she had done a good job. "Brutus and Rocky found it a while ago, when we were out exercising. They went missing and I thought I had lost them. I called and I called to no avail. They had never done this before. So, I went searching for them. I was nearly at my wits' end when they reemerged. Being curious to see what they, had found. I followed them back inside."

"Too bad there wasn't another exit; it would make a good escape route." Freya stated wistfully.

"The cavern beyond goes way back. I could explore more of the cavern next time I take Brutus and Rocky out for exercise." Pohla volunteered.

"That would be a good idea, Pohla! Thank you for volunteering, but you be sure to be careful. I will not lose another sister." Freya gave Pohla another reassuring hug.

"Do not worry, Freya, Brutus and Rocky would not let anything harm me." Pohla said.

"You are probably right but I still want you to be careful," Freya took one last look around. "Right! Come on now; we should be getting back. The others will be worrying." They then carefully exited the cave.

Fina, Tauna and Scara were waiting for them as they returned to their shelter. The trio had collected copious quantities of hardened leather, or cuirboilli, already cut to various sizes. All that was needed now was to shape and trim it before fitting it together.

The leather was made hard by impregnating it with wax. Boiling would soften it thereby making it pliable and easy to shape. It would be left to dry and harden. Once dry, it would retain this new shape. More trimming could be done to personalize the armor's fit.

Unfortunately, none of them had any real experience making armor: all they did have was a suit of orc armor to use for a pattern. So, it would be a bit of trial and error.

Freya looked over what her sisters had retrieved. "Yes, Scara, you were right. This should do nicely." She nodded in approval. "Pohla has found us a most excellent hiding place. She will be responsible for moving all our supplies there."

This assignment of duties did not seem to bother anyone, which was not surprising considering lugging all that gear would be a lot of work, not to mention risky.

Summer was winding down when Freya finally felt they were ready to escape. Autumn was coming to the Frontier. The leaves, once green from summer's sun, were shifting to the yellows and reds of autumn. The days were getting shorter and there was a chill to the night air.

It had taken longer than Freya would have liked to collect the vital supplies they needed to manage a successful escape but now they all had good, warm traveling clothes, a set of hardened leather armor, short swords, bows and shields.

In Freya's mind, there was only one last thing to do—pick the appropriate moment to escape. Then fate intervened. A major raid was announced, Kemac had finally decided it was time to deal with an annoying neighbor.

The raid would involve nearly all the forces of Chimera, except of course slaves like Freya and her sisters, which was a

ORC HAI!

good thing for they would have been lumped in with the orc contingent and considered cannon fodder.

The armory was opened. Every half-orc was armed with the best weapons and armor Kemac had to offer, while the orcs received the leftovers: no point in wasting resources on cannon fodder.

For Freya, this was the best outcome possible. The settlement and compounds would be virtually abandoned, leaving only a tiny disgruntled garrison behind, consisting entirely of human guardsman. Freya decided there would never be a better chance to escape.

In the confusion and rush to outfit every orc and half-orc, it was easy for a couple of light crossbows along with some armor (mostly light, scale and a few pairs of plate greaves and vambraces) to go missing. The sisters even managed to pilfer other small items to bolster their supplies and chances.

The night after the orcs and half-orcs marched out, and with the settlement in near darkness, Freya and her sisters prepared to escape.

Freya had Pohla lead her band out of their shelter and across the compound. She skillfully led them past the pens, which had until recently housed the hunting hounds, then onward to the stockade wall.

Once more, Pohla manipulated the timber pole to let them pass through.

When everyone was through, she repositioned the pole, hiding their exit point. This accomplished, Pohla led them to her secret entrance and the passage into the cave with its cavern beyond.

Pohla lit the lamp she had carefully prepared. As each of the other sisters entered, they gasped in astonishment.

"Wow!" was all Scara could muster.

"This is amazing, Pohla!" Fina added.

"Great place!" Tauna commented.

They all took in the cave with its five carefully arranged piles of equipment then noticed the immense cavern beyond.

In point of fact, the cavern led deep into the mountain and Pohla had been able to explore much of it while on the pretense of exercising Brutus and Rocky. So far, she had not yet found another exit but was confident that one was there.

Freya had been here before and knew how the cave and cavern could distract but her priority was to get everyone moving. "Suit up and put on only your hardened leather armor. Leave the scale in your packs!" She ordered.

Pohla had methodically and carefully sorted their supplies into five even piles, one personalized pile for each of them, clearly identified by certain personal items.

Each sister checked their kit and packs to be sure all was correct. Then, working in pairs, they helped each other into their armor. Freya was pleased with how well they worked together and she was impressed by Pohla's attention to detail in preparing everyone's gear, armor and weapons. She hoped the others also appreciated Pohla's efforts.

It was while she was in this contemplative mood that she realized just how much they looked like the orcs they despised. This should not have been a surprise considering they were outfitted in orc-style armor.

ORC HAI!

This mistake was understandable for the only example of armor they could scavenge and copy was of orc manufacture. Even their size did nothing to deter that image.

She would have to do something about that the first chance they got: of all the creatures she least wished to be mistaken for, an orc would top the list. But there was nothing she could do about their appearance right now: it was time to move on. "Is everybody all set?"

There was a series of head nods.

Those bobbing heads alerted her to another problem: visibility! These helmets, though affording good protection, provided atrocious vision and, currently, vision was more important than protection. So, the decision was obvious.

"I cannot see anything with this helmet on. Take them off until we need them!" Freya ordered.

Her sisters seemed happy with the idea and removed their helmets.

"Pohla, you will take the lead as you have explored the cavern ahead," Freya said. "Scara, you cover Pohla. I will bring up the rear."

As the sisters formed up, Fina grabbed the small oil lamp and fell in right behind Scara. The little oil lamp would be of assistance in the velvety blackness of the cavern.

Their night vision was fine but a little light was helpful and comforting. Of the five, Scara possessed the best night vision, probably due to the fact she had the most orc traits. Their marching order resolved, Pohla led them into the cavern.

3

At first, the going was easy: the terrain under foot relatively smooth as there was a layer of sand on the cavern floor. Pohla had left marks, in her previous explorations, to assist in guiding them through the maze of passages; now these markings kept them from straying off the path.

Soon their way became more rugged, forcing them to weave around a number of obstacles. The ceiling began to descend upon them and only then did it become obvious to Freya the passage was descending.

In fact, it was barely perceptible that is why they had come so far before Freya realized it. Then, just as she did, the trail leveled off.

The passage began to ascend again: a slow and gradual incline, much like their descent, saw the ceiling once again begin to disappear overhead.

Still, the sisters trudged on, with the only sounds being the swish of cloth on leather and the echo of their boots. The passage of time was hard to judge down here in the darkness and, after what seemed like an eternity, Freya decided to call a halt to the march for a rest.

"How much further?" Tauna grumbled as they sat down for a break and to munch on dried meat jerky and warm mead or water. To call it beef jerky would be stretching the truth.

"Oh, Tauna! We have only started." Scara chastised her.

"But my feet hurt!" Tauna rubbed her feet.

"Tauna, let me see your feet!" Freya ordered and Tauna complied, showing Freya her swollen feet. Freya studied them briefly then picked up Tauna's boots to examine them. "These are too small! Why did you not choose something larger?"

"Those were all I could find." Tauna sulked, as though a scolded child.

"They will need to be replaced," Freya pronounced. "Tauna, do you have some other footwear?"

"Just my compound sandals."

Not ideal, Freya thought, but they would have to do. "All right, use those until we can find you something better."

Pohla had waited patiently until Freya finished, then addressed Tauna's query. "Not much further now. Soon we will come to a stretch of the passage where water drips down creating round fang-like rocks. They stretch down from above while similar rocks rise from the floor to meet them. Some even touch each other; they are really quite beautiful. Beyond that, you will begin to feel the faint trace of fresh air. We follow that to the exit."

Pohla neglected to mention that she had not actually seen that exit. A fact only Freya knew, but she had instructed Pohla to not mention that to the others.

Freya knew she was taking a chance but it was a calculated risk based on

ORC HAI!

Pohla's information. Freya's gut had told her this was the correct course of action: so far, Pohla had been right. Sure, it was taking a risk but life was full of risks, especially for runty half-orc mongrels.

Freya let the others rest for a while longer as she massaged and tended Tauna's feet. Once she was satisfied Tauna's feet were taken care of, Freya settled on a quick bite of food and water before rousing her sisters to go. "Up, up! We cannot lay around here forever. Up! We must be off."

There were no complaints and Pohla once more took the lead and, after a short distance, the sound of dripping water could be heard. Only a short time later, Pohla spied water droplets falling from the cavern's ceiling far overhead and this moisture began to make the stone floor slippery.

Cone-shaped stalactites began to appear high above them, reaching down from the ceiling, while stalagmites rose up to meet them. These new formations sparkled in the light from the small lamp. None of them knew what a stalactite or stalagmite was but were awed by their appearance.

As Freya gazed up at them, a movement caught her eye. Curious, she focused on the movement and, to her horror, a stone broke loose and fell. She immediately realized it would hit either Pohla or Scara and shouted a warning as she dashed forward.

They looked up at her warning but Scara was the first to react. She shoved Pohla forward then used her shield to protect herself, deflecting the stalactite to the side.

Luckily, the stalactite only grazed her shield before impacting with a terrible crash onto the stone floor. Even so, Scara's shield received considerable damage. It now had a deep gouge in the wood and metal that ran from top to bottom.

"Good job, Scara! Are you all right?" Freya asked upon arriving.

"I am fine. I got lucky but my shield took a beating. Falling rocks! Really!" Scara surveyed her damaged shield.

"We will have to be more careful!" Freya advised.

"I'm fine too!" Pohla chimed in, picking herself up.

"Sorry, Pohla!" Freya rushed over to give her a quick examination.

Then, to their amazement, the stalactite looked up at them with a pair of beady black eyes and fixed them with an evil glare. The creature slowly began to right itself and began to slither away much like a snail.

"What is that thing?" Tauna asked.

"Who cares. Kill it!" Scara shouted.

What they had mistaken for a stalactite was really some kind of parasitic subterranean mollusk. Fortunately, on the cavern floor, the creature was so slow and cumbersome it was virtually harmless. Circling the parasite, the sisters stabbed and hacked at it, searching for a weak spot.

After a series of ineffective slashes and stabs, Freya realized their weapons were pretty much useless against the creature's shell. She called a halt to the attacks. An unpleasant thought came to her and she quickly looked up.

"Where there was one, there could be more of these creatures up there. So, keep a sharp eye out!"

With sudden inspiration, Freya readied her weapon. She and Scara must have had the same thought for together they thrust their short swords into the creature's eyes.

ORC HAI!

They rammed the blades as deep as they could, using their full body weight. The beast shuddered to a halt and died. With a whoop of triumph, the pair yanked out their swords as their shouts echoed around the cavernous passage.

All this time, Fina had been scanning the cavern ceiling for movement and she suddenly gasped. "Freya, we have movement all over the ceiling. I count at least twelve more."

"Twelve! Pohla, where have you led us!" Tauna pointed an accusing finger at Pohla and gave her a sharp look.

"Those were not here when I last came this way. None tried to fall on me or Brutus and Rocky!" Pohla shouted back in an angry retort.

"Well, how did they get here?" Scara scanned the ceiling. She was perhaps a little more sensitive than the others as her shield still bore the scar of deflecting one of the creatures.

"Enough!" Freya commanded. "It does not matter how they got here, they are here now and we will have to deal with them. Now silence! We know what to look for now so we should be able to avoid them," She paused. "Come on, let's go!"

Pohla and Scara set out with a more cautious pace and a fearful eye to the ceiling. Fortunately, the creatures were terribly slow and their only real advantage was surprise.

It was while making a detour that Pohla came across the dead body that had obviously been impaled by one of those piercing creatures. "Freya, there is a dead man-child here." Pohla called out.

This body puzzled her, for she had been down this way only a week ago and Brutus and Rocky would surely have found him. So, it was obvious to her this body and these piercer creatures had not been down here then.

"Why does he have hairy feet and no footwear?" Fina asked as she approached.

"What?" The others replied in near unison.

"Hairy feet!" Fina pointed to the body's feet.

The others had assumed they were just the remains of furry boots.

"Well, if it is not a man-child, what is it?" Scara asked, looking to Freya for answers.

"Beats me!" Freya was just as baffled as the rest. Not surprising considering their limited experience with other species.

"He was not here a week ago," Pohla explained. "Brutus and Rocky would have found him."

"Search him and his belongings. Take whatever we can use. He will not need them now. Who knows, maybe it will shed some light on who and what he was doing in here."

The bodies belongings consisted of a pack with extra clothing, which was too small for any of them to wear. There was a purse on his belt containing two gold pieces, seven silver pieces and fourteen copper pieces; also, a very good quality short sword and scabbard made by a fine craftsman.

A further search through his pack revealed an array of durable pots and pans. Among these was an assortment of cooking utensils and various spices. Last was a large coil of strong, finely made rope, perhaps fifty feet long, and an assortment of food. There were potatoes, wild mushrooms, rice, smoked meat, dried and sugared fruit and some kind of bread wrapped in leaves.

ORC HAI!

While Pohla and Tauna searched the little one's body, Freya decided to study the slow-moving parasitic piercing creatures around them. Fina joined her in keeping a sharp eye on the piercers, the name they were now thinking of calling them.

To Fina, the piercers appeared to have stopped moving, so she moved away from Freya for a better look. This was when she found a second body, an elf she suspected. Although Fina had never seen an elf before, she had heard descriptions of them and they matched this one. The elf had long straight blonde hair and fine facial features, which were partially spoiled by an ugly wound to his throat and shoulder from a piercer but, unlike the little one, he was not fed on.

He was dressed in clothes that would easily blend in with the forest. Beside him lay a bow and quiver, empty of arrows. Fina looked out across the cavern to see what he could possibly be shooting at but it was too far and too dark. This baffled her.

"Over here! I found another one. An elf, I think." Fina called out.

That got her sisters' attention. They immediately abandoned any further search of the first body and came over.

"An elf!" They all whispered in awe, staring at the body.

None of them had ever seen one. Although they had heard plenty of horror stories, often grizzly accounts of fair-haired elves slaughtering orcs by the thousand with weapons, which burned an orc at the touch.

All orcs hated elves but were instinctively scared to death of them. Before Freya could stop her, Pohla reached down to touch the elf. "Pohla, no!" But it was too late.

When nothing harmful happened to Pohla, she let out her breath, which, until then, she had not realized she had been holding. Looking around, Freya realized she was not the only one anticipating something bad to happen.

"Pohla, that was very risky. Are you, all right?" Freya asked.

"I am fine, Freya," Pohla replied and when Freya continued to look at her concerned, she added, "really."

"Okay, Pohla, then you get to search him. Take whatever you can but be careful." Freya was unwilling to let anyone else touch the elf; those stories of frightful injuries still too clear in her mind.

"Spread out! There may be more of them. And keep an eye out for those damn piercers. I will cover Pohla." Freya now suspected why the piercers had appeared here.

"His quiver is empty, Freya, so who was he was shooting at?" Pohla added.

No sooner had they began to search when Scara piped up. "Two more of the small ones over here and one was hit by an arrow," she reported. "An orc arrow!" The other was probably carrying him when one of those piercer creatures got them both and, Freya, there are also more than a few orc arrows over here."

"Just great!" Freya groaned. "These four must have been pursued into the cavern system by wild orc. We will have to be more careful; there may be more orc about. Scara, you know the drill: search them. Pohla, are you done yet?"

"Just about!" Pohla replied almost cheerfully. With great reverence, Pohla had been carefully searching the handsome elf then removing whatever she found. What she had procured was a fine bow with its empty quiver, a fine pair of curved throwing knives, a gray cloak and blanket and a money purse containing a number of silver pieces.

ORC HAI!

The bow and blanket she exchanged with her own. Then, with her old blanket, she covered his body.

Meanwhile, Scara's search had turned up two more money purses and a pair of excellent short swords, similar to the one Pohla had procured.

There was also more food, two wooden pipes with pouches of pipe-weed, plus two blankets and bedrolls (unfortunately the blanket and bedrolls were too small for any of them to use). Scara had also gathered a handful of orc arrows.

"Waste not, want not." Scara selected the best and tossed the rest.

What seemed truly odd to Freya, however, was that none of the bodies showed any signs of desecration or looting commonly performed by orc on an enemy. So, what happened to the orcs? Where did they go? Could those piercers have scared them off? Unlikely, she thought, but a riddle for another time.

With these tasks completed, Freya called them all together. Since the encounter with the piercers, they had been making their way cautiously, often not very close together. Freya now felt that should stop.

"With the possibility of wild orcs around, we should stay closer together for support in case of an attack," Freya ordered. "But first, I have a little bit of business to attend to."

They had always shared pretty much everything. Of course, there was never much to share. As Freya was now the unanimous leader, she had no intention of altering their "share and share alike" policy. The difference now was it was her responsibility to distribute the loot they had just acquired.

Freya's system was simple: money would be used for the group with perhaps a small portion distributed to each for personal use. While equipment would go to whomever was most suited to and capable of using said item.

She found herself with three excellent quality short swords, far better than anything they had. As she and Scara were the best swordswomen, followed next by Fina, this was who would get the new swords.

Pohla was best with a bow so she would keep the elf bow and elf knives. No one seemed to want them anyway. Everyone was still a little superstitious about touching them.

The better quality, cooking pots and utensils went to Tauna as she was the best cook. The various other supplies and food were spread among them.

Freya kept the money for a group pool to buy whatever the group needed if they could afford it. Their accumulated fortune tallied six gold, fifty silver and sixty-four copper pieces. A fortune for them as this was more money than they had ever seen before. Although, in the real world, it was really not much.

"We must be even more careful now. There are wild orcs about," she reminded them. "From here on, Scara and I will take the lead. Pohla you are with us. Fina and Tauna, stay close." Freya distributed their loot.

They left behind three old swords and a set of poor quality, cooking pots. No point carrying what you do not need, Freya reasoned. Unfortunately, the passage no longer seemed as magnificent: it took on a dangerous foreboding air. Each stalactite was a piercer and every shadow hid an orc archer.

4

Soon they began to find more orc arrows lying spent on the passage floor—many more orc arrows in fact; the best of which Scara picked up and added to her short bow quiver. Some of her sisters followed her lead.

The fletching or feathering told the story of these arrows. Wild orcs used whatever materials were available; whereas organized orcs, like the ones at Chimera, used a uniform material and pattern to identify their allegiance.

In no time at all they appeared to have slipped ahead of the slow-moving piercers. It was about here they came across the body of an orc then close by another. Both had been killed by an elf arrow: one in the face, the other in the throat; both died writhing in agony. These two orcs were no better equipped than the sisters were, so all they took from them were their purses and there was little enough in those. The grand total was twelve copper pieces combined.

Pohla, however, took the opportunity to collect both elf arrows, clean them and place them in her quiver. None of her sisters would dare to touch them. She then looked back in the direction of where they found the elf.

The distance was unbelievable: no one could possibly shoot accurately from that far. So perhaps the stories about elves were true.

"Freya, how could he shoot this far?" Fina, too, followed Pohla's gaze.

"He was an elf, that's how!" Scara explained briskly.

A few paces further, three more orcs lay twisted in agony, all killed by a single elf arrow. The sisters only stopped briefly to collect anything worthwhile, which turned out to be their money purses, which, by the feel of them, contained only a meager quantity of copper pieces.

Soon, more and more orc arrows began to appear all over the passage and amongst them lay numerous dead, orcs. The majority of the dead, twelve in fact, died from an elf arrow. Arrows which Pohla enthusiastically collected. Her quiver was now filling. Fourteen splendid arrows, she thought, happily patting her quiver.

The pickings were no better with this lot but they did manage to acquire fifty-four more copper pieces. Well, at least now Freya knew what the elf was shooting at and why there were no wild orcs still about.

Between the orcs the elf had killed and those piercers, had got, that probably frightened them off. Wild orc never had much moral fortitude in the face of danger.

It also appeared the stories were true—elves never missed. This elf must have been protecting the little ones as they had fled into the caverns to escape from the orc.

Still, something seemed wrong to Freya, who now had more questions than answers; like why would an elf be traveling with these little ones, what were they anyway, and why would the elf flee from so few, orcs?

At least one thing was confirmed; there was an exit from the cavern system. But she had no more time to dwell on this as Fina interrupted her thoughts.

"Hey, there is another body down here!" Fina shouted after a quick look down into a small chasm just off their chosen path.

Coming over for a look, Freya spied the body of an old man on a ledge quite far down. He was dressed all in gray robes with long graying hair and a gray beard. Numerous orc arrows were sticking in him and he looked rather frail lying down there.

Things were getting odder and odder, Freya thought. There seemed little point in climbing down to search him. It would be far too risky and take too long. "Let's go: there is nothing we can do for him!" Freya ordered.

The sisters continued up the passage and, in no time, more and more orc bodies began to appear—a lot more orc bodies. Ahead, the dead were piled on top of one another as if they had clambered over their own dead in an attempt to get too or away from something but were cut down in the process.

Cut down was an appropriate description for there was blood and gore scattered everywhere. Freya and her sisters cautiously circled the carnage, trying to make sense of it.

Eventually, out of frustration, Freya clambered up on top of the pile. From there she realized the orc dead circled two dead men and a dead dwarf, who had fought back-to-back until the bitter end.

Both men wielded mighty broadswords while the dwarf had held a deadly two-handed, double-bladed battleaxe. You could see the carnage left by the dwarf's two-handed battleaxe: limbs severed and scattered about, decapitations, even bodies sliced in two.

The trio, overcome by sheer weight of numbers but still managing to kill all that faced them before finally succumbing from too many wounds.

One of the men carried an oval shield on his back and curled horn at his side. He had suffered many wounds, although his armor and shield had stopped a great many more blows. In his hand was a beautiful broadsword.

The second man was dressed in green and brown. He was dark haired and scruffy in appearance, although his handsome features showed through. In one hand, he clutched an impressive looking broadsword. In the other, an amulet made of a shiny, silvery metal.

His final act had been to decapitate the orc chieftain who was a huge, fat beast and, by killing him, he would have demoralized and routed any surviving orcs causing them to flee in panic.

Freya believed the man would have lived long enough to see the effect of his handiwork before his injuries took him. Thus, the reason the bodies were not desecrated or defiled. It was beginning to make sense to Freya but she still had some questions.

Appalled at the carnage, Freya had her sisters begin to try to get a count of the dead. It was hard to get an accurate count with all the severed limbs and they gave up at sixty-four, although there were clearly many, many more buried under

ORC HAI!

the pile of bodies that they could not count, and Freya was not going to have them dig through the pile.

"Sixty-four dead orcs and those are what we can count!" Scara crowed.

"And that is not counting those down the passage!" Fina countered.

"Good riddance!" Scara added.

Looking ahead, Freya could see more: a great many more. "Okay let's see what we can find."

The orc dead rendered a large quantity of copper pieces and a few pieces of usable plate armor, specifically greaves and vambraces. The orc chieftain yielded more loot than all the other orcs combined: five gold pieces and three gemstones. Freya took one of the beautifully made broadswords for herself and tossed Scara the other, who immediately tested it for feel and balance by swinging it around.

"I like it!" She smiled.

They passed off their short swords to Pohla and Tauna who tossed away their old orc blades.

The dwarf's double-bladed battleaxe was not suited to Freya or any of her sisters' abilities. It was too heavy and awkward for any of them to wield effectively. Still, Freya decided to take it along rather than leave it for orc scavengers. She also acquired quite a number of gold pieces from his purse.

Both the men carried fancy daggers, bedrolls and blankets, all worth keeping. On the hand of the man dressed in brown and green was a fancy ring made of that same silvery metal as the amulet.

Unknown to the sisters, this was a magic ring and if any had put it on, it would have immediately adjusted to fit the wearer's finger. The amulet clutched in his other hand was too tempting and Scara was first to try to retrieve it, but it burnt her the second she touched it.

"Yikes!" Scara jerked her hand back and the pendant dropped to the ground.

"That is of elf design, unless I am mistaken." Freya ventured.

"Thanks for the heads up," Scara cursed shaking her hand. "Pohla, you pick it up."

Pohla looked at Scara dubiously then to Freya who nodded her concurrence. She then reached down and picked it off the ground and nothing happened to her.

"It is beautiful." Pohla examined the piece.

"Good. Pohla, you may keep it until we decide what to do with it. Oh, and see if you can get that ring too." Freya suggested and no one protested after Scara's experience.

Freya was feeling bad about all the looting they were doing. Well, really only bad about taking from these brave souls then leaving them for the scavengers. She was beginning to feel a little like a scavenger herself, when one of those scavengers arrived—a cave lion searching for a meal.

A warning shout from Fina and a roar from behind her made Freya drop and roll. Even so, a big hairy paw managed to graze her armor. Scara ran over with her shield, only slowing to snap up a spear.

Freya had no time to wonder why the big cat had bypassed all the easy meals nearer the entrance as it leapt at her and Scara.

There was a distinct twang of a bowstring and the cat rolled hitting the ground dead before skidding to a halt just short of them. An elf arrow was buried deep in its chest. The arrow ruptured its heart, tearing through its lungs, killing it instantly.

Freya and Scara quickly looked around for the source and there stood Pohla, elf bow in hand and with another arrow notched and ready to fly if need be. Freya waved a hand in thanks as she breathed a sigh of relief. Another elf was the last thing she wished to see right now.

This encounter with the lion did however convince her they must do something to honor these fallen comrades. She also knew time was of the essence if they wanted to escape, but she believed the delay was worth it. There was no way to dig a grave in the stone floor.

"We are going to raise a cairn over these brave companions!" Freya decided. She then had her sisters move the two men together and laid out side by side with their arms folded across their chests.

"Good. Now place the dwarf next to them," Freya instructed.

That accomplished, she folded his arms across his chest like his companions. Lain together, they looked quite peaceful.

"I will stay to guard the bodies," Freya said. "Scara, you take the others and go bring back the elf and the three little ones."

5

Upon their return, Freya had the four laid out to either side of the first three. While they were away, she debated this next recovery, and in the end, decided it would be the right thing to do, but this one would be the most challenging.

To get to the old man in gray, someone would have to be lowered down with a rope. Once on the ledge, they would have to tie it around the old man so he could be hauled up. Then the rope would need to be re-lowered to haul up whomever went down.

"Right, who feels like a climb?" Freya asked

Fina was the best climber but not the only volunteer. Besides Fina, both Pohla and Scara volunteered and this surprised her. In the end, she selected Fina and was pleasantly surprised at how quickly the job was accomplished.

Once the eight were laid out together and their remaining pieces of equipment placed with them, Freya had them covered with multiple layers of shields. On top of this, the sisters piled as many orc weapons as they could collect.

Finally satisfied with a job well done, Freya called a break. They were all tired but they still had enough energy to set up a proper camp. As they relaxed around their camp, the sisters experienced a feeling of pride in what they had accomplished. Something they had never felt back in Chimera.

"Good job, everyone, and a very profitable first day."

"Night." Scara corrected.

"Are you sure?" Freya questioned and Scara tilted her head and gave Freya, her obviously look. "Fine, night. I have therefore decided to reward each of us with fifty copper pieces," Freya continued then counted out the coins.

Her announcement created tremendous excitement. It was not a lot of money but to them who had never had any money, it seemed a fortune.

"This is your personal spending money for when we reach a town." Freya explained.

"Will we really be welcome in any town?" Scara voiced what was probably on all their minds.

"I have done a lot of thinking about that and money is always welcome if we are not. We are not rich by any means but we have a tidy sum," She held up four purses. "We have thirty-one gold, fifty silver and two-hundred-ten copper pieces, plus these three gemstones and a ring. Certainly, enough to keep us from begging for quite some time!" That brought a cheer from her sisters.

"A town is the only place we can find the worth of these gemstones and learn about the ring. I fear, however, we must be careful, for not everyone can be trusted," There was a chorus of laughs at that. "It would also be prudent for us to look a little less orcish."

"But we cannot change what we are!" Tauna protested.

ORC HAI!

"It is not our looks I speak of, but our clothes and our armor. Just have a look at us. I do not want us killed at first sight because we look like orcs." Freya demonstrated her meaning by doing a slow pirouette for effect.

Scara, Fina, Pohla and Tauna all looked at her then around at each other, and understood what Freya meant for they looked like five orcs.

"First impressions are important. If you look like an orc, you will be treated like one. So, if we do not want to be hunted down, we must change our appearance. Our lives may depend on it!" Freya emphasized her concern and finally there were nods of agreement from all.

"Do not worry, Freya; I will just put a bag over my head!" Scara joked and they all laughed.

"Scara brings up a good point. How do we deal with our looks, Freya?" Fina asked for they had little experience in the ways of the world.

"We have seen what men wear. Surely women warriors must wear something similar." Freya reasoned.

"The women in the compound did not." Fina pointed out.

"Nor did that evil hag, Helene." Tauna volunteered with a shudder.

"Yes, but they were not warriors." Freya countered.

"Perhaps women do not fight." Tauna speculated.

"No, I have heard the men speak of women warriors." Scara jumped in.

"Scara is right. I have heard those stories too and not the wildly exaggerated drunken tales." Pohla finally piped up.

"Yes, Pohla, you and Scara are right. That is why I think it is so important that we alter our appearance to look more like man folk."

Suddenly, in a flash of insight, Freya had an idea. "Color," she shouted then suddenly realized her sisters thought her daft. "Color," she said again more calmly for it was now clear to her.

"The orcs and half-orcs in Chimera dressed only in dull browns or blacks, even these, wild orc dressed the same. However, the eight we just interred were attired in different styles and colors. Even the guards at Chimera wore uniforms in brighter colors."

"Yes! And those uniforms are far better both in cut and craftsmanship." Tauna added. Being an excellent seamstress, she had made or repaired many of those same uniforms.

"Not to mention armor and weapons." Scara waved her impressive new broadsword.

"Scara and Tauna are absolutely correct and, with a few modifications and these new weapons, we should be able to pass among the places of men." It was quite a reasoned observation for one such as Freya, a half-breed orc.

Freya and her sisters had been part of a grandiose crossbreeding experiment. An experiment to breed a bigger, smarter and tougher half-orc. At least two of those traits were passed along to them.

Still, Kemac did not see it, too concerned with size and sex so he considered them failures and rejected them putting them to work as slaves.

Now, however, the truly successful product of those experiments, were escaping to freedom and that fool Kemac did not have a clue.

ORC HAI!

Freya turned to her sisters who were looking at her expectantly. "We have money, which will allow us to alter our attire and appearance to fit better into the world of men. After all, Tauna made and repaired most of the uniforms in Chimera."

Freya knew Pohla would have the easiest time passing for a woman for she was the most like her mother. Freya and Fina were a close second. Tauna would be considered homely at best, but Scara would take a bit of work to ever pass for anything other than half-orc. At least now they all understood what was needed.

"Pohla, you killed the lion, it is yours to do with as you please. Perhaps it would make a good start to modifying your attire." Freya added.

The sisters all knew how to skin, clean and treat an animal hide to ensure its usability. This they had learned back at the compound. One of the enumerable tasks required of them.

Now, while Pohla began the task of skinning, cleaning and preparing the cat hide, her sisters began to prepare a meal.

As the thought of food began to enter heads, Tauna piped up. "I wonder what lion tastes like?"

"I hear it tastes like chicken." Scara joked and they all laughed.

"Well, it would be a shame to waste good meat. Travel rations are fine but—" Tauna mused wistfully.

"Tauna, you think too much with your belly." Fina teased.

"We have not been gone long enough to get sick of travel rations yet and I would bet that meat is pretty tough and stringy." Freya added into the laughter.

"I could boil it soft," Tauna countered and there was more laughter. "Laugh now but when food gets scarce," Tauna's voice trailed off at their looks.

"We do not have the time to waste on that. We have to get as far from Chimera as we can as fast as we can!" Freya intervened to take the sting off the laughter.

Tauna's reaction was understandable when you considered their diet back in Chimera. For them, food was pretty much anything they could steal or scrounge, which was often almost nothing.

The order of the day was to take whatever scraps from the kitchen and dining hall you could find. They supplemented this with whatever they could catch, most often rats. There were always lots and lots of rats. This was the way of things for the slaves.

When Pohla finished working with the cat's hide, she rolled it up, leaving the final treatment for later. She then tossed the remainder of the cat's carcass down the fissure they had retrieved the old gray-haired man from before rejoining her companions.

There she sat down to eat a meal of dried meat and unleavened bread. Not particularly tasty but she had eaten far worse. In fact, they had all eaten far worse.

"Anyone want to try some of this dried fruit?" Tauna held up a piece of what looked like a sugared apple. "Or this? It is some kind of bread." she displayed a package wrapped in leaves.

"You try it first." Scara proposed.

Tauna shrugged and chose the dried fruit. "Mmmm! This is really good!" And she took another bite.

ORC HAI!

With Tauna's taste test of approval, they all selected a piece and it was definitely the best portion of the meal. No one decided to try the bread.

"Once we get outside, we can see about catching some game." Freya suggested.

Before the meal was finished, Freya set up a guard rotation and once that was accomplished, they all settled in for a little rest, with the exception of Scara who had asked for first watch. Some just rested; some slept.

6

They had been traveling all night and well into the next day, although you would not know it: underground day and night blended into one.

As another night approached, Freya roused them. It was time once more to move on. The five had a quick snack then packed up. Pohla and Scara took the lead followed by Fina and Tauna while Freya brought up the rear.

Everyone kept a wary eye to the ceiling for any sign of those piercers. Remarkably, the ceiling remained clear of that threat.

Certain that the exit was close, Pohla picked up the pace as all the while they passed the dead bodies of more orcs. Some had fallen to an elf arrow (often these were in pairs impaled by a single arrow), while others had fallen to a sword slash or thrust and others were obviously cloven apart by that mighty battleaxe the dwarf wielded.

They looted these bodies of money as they came across them. In this way, they counted another seventeen dead orcs and pocketed another fifty copper pieces.

Meanwhile, Pohla happily recovered four more elf arrows. Her quiver now held eighteen arrows and their fortune now at thirty-one gold, fifty silver and, two- hundred-sixty copper pieces, plus three gemstones. And that was not counting the fifty copper pieces each sister received from Freya as a reward.

All in all, it had been a good adventure so far and the increase in fresh air signified that the exit was close by. Fina reached forward and tapped Scara on the shoulder.

"I can see the way out just ahead." She whispered a warning.

Obviously, night had fallen, hiding the exit from most of them. So it was by mere chance that they emerged from the mountain passage into darkness. This suited Freya just fine.

Freya and her sisters were as comfortable in the night as the daylight. Freya knew they would have to alter this pattern very soon but, for now, they could not afford the delay.

Pohla and Scara stopped well back of the way out and waved Freya forward.

Freya ordered the lamp to be put out as a precaution. They should not need it and, as the light was extinguished, they found that they did not.

Cautiously edging forward, Freya realized their way out resembled a bulging inverted V, perhaps twenty feet high at the apex and thirty feet wide at its base. She paused for she was in no hurry to dash out exposing them to the unknown.

Freya wished to avoid an ambush, however improbable, so she slipped to one side of the passage's exit for cover. Freya studied what lay ahead. She thought she could make out another body out there but could not identify what kind it was.

Seeing nothing else, Freya signaled for her sisters to come forward. Five sets of eyes were better than one. She felt the

ORC HAI!

others slip in beside her. Here they settled in quietly to watch in silence.

"I see nothing," Pohla whispered.

"Just more dead orcs," Fina finished for her.

"No man smells either," Scara added.

Scara had the best night vision and sense of smell of them all. This was a good sign as the wind was blowing their way, carrying with it all the scents of the night.

"Anything else? Anyone?" Freya asked. When nothing was forthcoming, Freya made the call. "All right then. Let's go. Everyone, keep your eyes open. Scara, you take the lead. Fina, Tauna right behind her. I will bring up the rear, Pohla, you are right in front of me."

Scara cautiously stepped out from the relative protection of the cavern's wall. Her eyes swept from left to right as she scanned for signs of trouble. Seeing none and smelling nothing, she advanced with the others following close behind.

The chilly night reminded them of the lateness of the season. There was a light cloud cover but the moon added a little illumination and, once outside, the group's excellent night vision improved remarkably and their surroundings sprang into clear focus.

Little did they know that they had emerged many miles away from Chimera, deep in the middle of the Ered Chimera mountain range. Their subterranean route had indeed been a shortcut.

When no ambush came, Scara increased the pace, passing a scattering of dead orcs, some they had seen from the cave mouth. They also collected another fifty copper pieces from the dead.

This section of the mountain range was steeper and rockier while tall conifer trees dotted the landscape. These were mighty firs and their numbers began to increase as they descended the mountain. Soon the firs would become a forest.

Scara was first to notice a change in the scent carried on the wind. "Hounds!" She simply stated. Then they could make out the faint sounds of howls and barks.

"How can they have caught up to us?" Freya cursed their bad luck.

"We are caught?" Tauna wailed.

"I will die before I go back!" Scara vowed.

"We will fight," Freya commanded and there was a chorus of agreements before Pohla piped up.

"Those are not our hounds!"

"Not our hounds? Are you sure, Pohla?" Freya asked.

"Of course. These are probably wolves or wild dogs hunting."

"Hunting? Hunting what?" Freya was concerned it might be them.

"Probably game. Deer most likely or even some of those wild orcs." Pohla advised.

"There cannot be too many of them left." Scara stated.

"Deer meat," Tauna began. "Perhaps we should check it out and steal some fresh meat."

This time, however, no one laughed at her suggestion. So, with no opposition and being a little curious herself, Freya decided they should check it out.

"Which way?" Freya asked Pohla and Scara. There was no hesitation from the pair: they pointed to the northwest. "Let's check it out. Lead on."

ORC HAI!

So off they headed in a northwesterly direction. Soon, the terrain became less rugged and they picked up the pace, the barking and growling increasing in volume and intensity.

"They have cornered something and it is putting up a fight. It must be a stag or a buck," Pohla theorized based on the sounds of the dogs. She had heard Brutus and Rocky make similar noises when hunting. "We are close—real close."

"Stick together," Freya said. "That way, we can protect each other better."

"Give the dogs plenty of room to run away." Pohla advised.

"Yes, we only want to drive them off!" Freya ordered.

Closer now, they advanced more slowly. They all wore hardened leather armor; some had iron greaves on their arms and vambraces on their legs. No one had donned their helmets. After all, these were just animals.

Of the five, only Pohla elected to draw her bow. With swords and shields at the ready, they charged out to chase off the pack.

Much to their surprise, the dogs had not cornered a stag but another of those little ones they had first thought of as children of men. But backed up against a pile of boulders a small figure was trying to fend off about fifteen wild dogs.

It was fortunate they could only attack him from the front. However, once he tired, or if a dog mounted those rocks behind him, he would be finished.

Almost as if the dogs had read Freya's mind, a dog suddenly appeared on the rocks above him. The elf bow sang as Pohla loosed an arrow to strike the dog before it could jump. The shot was true and the beast collapsed in a heap with an arrow piercing its heart. The dog then slid lifeless off the rock, startling the little fellow.

Fortunately for him, the other dogs were just as surprised and missed the opportunity it presented. Now the dogs hesitated in confusion. However, confusion was short lived, lasting mere seconds.

The pack still outnumbered this new prey almost three to one. In their eyes there was just more prey and instinct took over. They split up their attack, with a few continuing to attack the little fellow while the larger pack attacked Freya and her sisters.

A second dog made a lunging charge at the little one, but Pohla took him down. The little one waved his thanks. It was then that Pohla realized this small one was not a child but a half-sized adult.

Freya, Fina, Scara and Tauna were using their shields to form a protective wall against the dog's onslaught. One overly aggressive dog felt Scara's blade as she plunged it deep into his chest. It howled and died with a violent twitch.

While Scara's arm was exposed, another dog made a lunge for it, only to have Freya slice down on the back of its neck. Freya's broadsword tore through hide, meat, sinew and bone severing the beast's spine nearly decapitating it.

Pohla's bow sang twice more in rapid succession, taking down two more dogs. One dog, a huge beast, separated from the pack and began to circle the sisters. Fina realized the threat and kept an eye on the beast. This was probably the pack leader.

Suddenly, the beast saw an opportunity and leapt at Pohla's exposed back as she stood in the center of their little armored circle. Fina reacted immediately jumping up and using her shield to protect Pohla from the jumping animal. As she deflected the pack leader away, she rammed her short sword into its belly.

The dying dog landed safely outside their circle but Fina was knocked back into Pohla by the sheer weight of the impact with the inevitable result being they both went down in a tangle of limbs.

Near their breaking point and with the pack leader's death, the remaining pack was about to run away but became re-emboldened by Pohla and Fina falling. As the pair tried to disentangle themselves, the remaining dogs lunged to the attack.

This new attack was met with the flashing swords from Scara, Freya and Tauna. Two dogs died immediately one to Scara's broadsword and the other to Freya's, while Tauna managed to seriously wound a third.

With the attack blunted; the dogs had enough. Nine dogs were dead including the pack leader and, as their resolve faltered, a final lunge by Freya and Scara caused the remaining dogs to flee.

7

Fordoc thought he was a goner when he had become separated from his traveling companions by a large party of wild orcs. It was after managing to elude them, that a pack of wild dogs picked up his scent and chased him down, finally cornering him against this rockface.

Then, just when he thought it could not get any worse, a small party of orcs appeared. So, if the dogs did not get him the orcs certainly would. But, to his great surprise, the orcs began to attack the pack and twice their archer intervened to save his life. This action completely baffled him.

It was when the moonlight filtered through a break in the clouds that he realized this small band of orcs may not be orcs after all. The darkness and their attire that had led him to believe they were orcs. Now, in fact, they appeared to be females and not orcs as he first assumed but what were they.

There was one scary moment when two of the females went down to a leaping dog. One was the archer but, after a furious flourish of swords in which more dogs were killed, the remaining dogs took flight and he breathed a sigh of relief. It looked like he might just live—well, he hoped so.

Now, however, it was time to go and thank his (hopefully) saviors. Dusting himself off, he began to walk slowly over, picking his way around the dead dogs as he approached.

"Thank you! I thought I was done for." Fordoc extended a hand in gratitude and greetings.

Freya was so busy checking her sisters, ensuring no one was injured, she did not notice the little fellow approaching. In fact, she had forgotten all about the stranger.

Well, everyone had forgotten about him except for Pohla; she had been watching him approach. When he spoke, the others quickly turned around startled and brandishing swords in response.

Fordoc froze as they turned with their weapons at the ready. Suddenly, he was unsure again of their intentions and, for a brief moment, he thought, Oh, great out of the frying pan and into the fire.

Events had happened so fast and unexpectedly that, for the first time in a while, Freya was unsure how to proceed. Pohla stepped into this pause; she separated herself from the others and approached Fordoc.

"Hello. Thank you for saving my life." Fordoc began again hesitantly.

"You are welcome. Are you hurt?" Pohla noted he had a strange accent.

"No, only my pride I am afraid. I am Fordoc."

"I am Pohla," she took the cue and introduced herself before introducing her companions. "These are my sisters: Freya, Fina, Tauna and Scara,"

"Thank you all," Fordoc nodded gratefully to each one of them. He then reached out and touched her hand. "And a special thanks to you, Pohla. You saved my life."

As she blushed, Fordoc studied her features. She was taller than he was but short for a female of man folk. Not unpleasant to look at but not beautiful either. Only, there was something about her and her sisters. Something he could not put his finger on just yet.

Pohla felt her face heat in way she never had before. For her part, she had never received such attention and was baffled on how to react. It was here that Freya intervened.

"It was unwise of you to be out here alone. You may travel with us for a while if you wish." Freya now realized, as Pohla had, that this was no child or youngster, but an adult. But an adult what? Perhaps the stranger might be of assistance. At the very least he may draw attention away from them.

"Thank you for your kind offer, I would be most pleased to accept it. I was separated from my companions when we were attacked by wild orcs and, while trying to find them, those wolves found me." Fordoc gave an abridged version of his misadventures. He was not entirely confident those dwarves would bother to look for him.

As he explained his situation, Pohla was getting a very bad feeling. She turned to look at her sisters to see if they were coming to the same conclusion. Obviously, Freya had and, with a nod, gave Pohla the okay to break the bad news.

"Your companions—there were eight of them?" Pohla asked, then saw him shake his head.

"No, my companions were three halflings and twelve dwarves." Fordoc pointed out to the relief of Pohla and her sisters.

"Halflings? What are halflings?" Freya interrupted.

"I am a halfling; that is what my people are called by men folk. We are sometimes called little folk." He was puzzled they did not know this.

Freya filed this information away. They had never heard of a halfling before. Then who were the dead companions they interred in the cavern?

"Who were these fellows and where did you see them?" Fordoc asked, curious about why they had asked?

"We came across their bodies only a day ago. Three others of your kind, an elf, a dwarf, two men at arms and an old man. They had been dead a couple of days. A large orc raiding party pursued them into a cavern system. They had killed over one hundred orcs before being overcome. There was also some kind of parasite that looked like a rock and falls from the roof of the cavern. They try to impale whatever walks below them. We erected a cairn over their bodies for the ground was too hard to bury them. Hopefully this will protect their bodies from animals or being defiled. We interred them with most of their belongings—"

"Pohla!" Freya interrupted her with a shake of her head.

"You thought they were my companions?" Fordoc finally understood their behavior.

"Yes! Now if you still wish to travel with us, we must be off!" Freya took charge again.

"Thank you. You are most kind. I believe I will take you up on your kind offer." Fordoc had enough of traveling alone.

ORC HAI!

"Scara, you have the lead." Freya began.

"What about the fur?" Tauna asked. She was about to add and the meat but the incident with the lion was fresh in her mind so she remained quiet.

"Leave it. It is probably flea ridden!" Freya ordered. "Fina, you follow Scara, Pohla, you and Fordoc in the middle with Tauna. I will bring up the rear. Let's go!" Freya finished with a clap of her hands.

Fordoc almost immediately had trouble keeping up, even with Pohla and Tauna's help. After about an hour of struggling in the semi-darkness, he began to whisper to Pohla. "Pohla, you and your sisters travel well at night. Do you often travel at night?"

"We have just escaped our bonds and must put some distance between us and our captors at Chimera. We escaped under the cover of darkness and have been running ever since to avoid pursuit." Pohla explained quietly.

"You were captured in a raid then?" Fordoc was shocked.

"Not us but our mothers. We were born into slavery." Pohla admitted.

"That's terrible!" He was appalled, then realized where he was. He had spoken too loud and Scara gave him a chastising look. "Sorry," he tried to apologize for his indiscretion. Pohla gave him a forgiving smile. "But you said you were sisters?" He shifted back to a whisper.

"We are sisters: sisters in misery. Freya and Fina are the only true sisters, siblings of the same mother."

"I see. Sisters, as in a sisterhood. Like Amazons," Fordoc hypothesized.

"Sisterhood, I like that. Yes, a sisterhood in a way. I will suggest it to Freya."

Pohla paused at something else he said. "Amazons? What are Amazons?"

"Amazons are women who choose to live apart from men. They are usually warriors." He explained.

"Are all women fighters Amazons?"

"I am not an expert on Amazons but, no. There are women warriors who fight alongside men and these are not considered Amazons. Real Amazons stick together in a sisterhood ruled by female leaders. They usually only mix with men to mate, or so the stories go."

This gave Pohla a lot to think about but she was extremely curious about Fordoc and his people. He had mentioned that men called his kind halflings so perhaps Fordoc was a half-breed like them.

"None of us recognized your kind. What are halflings?" she began hesitantly, fearing he might take offense.

Instead, his expression brightened. "As I said, my people are called halflings. Men often refer to us as little folk because of our size. Not to be mistaken for brownies or leprechauns. We halflings are something completely different." Fordoc explained cheerfully.

So, he was not a half-breed like she hoped. She felt she must be truthful and let the cards fall where they may to judge how others were going to react to them. Afterall, he would realize it soon enough.

"Fordoc," Pohla began nervously, "there is something you should know."

ORC HAI!

"Pohla! No!" Freya had heard much of the hushed conversation and now intervened, fearing the result.

"Freya, he should know," Pohla insisted

"What should I know? That you are more than you appear?" Fordoc interrupted.

He had suspected for a while that these women were not all they appeared to be. At first glance, they looked like orcs but clearly Pohla was not. To his eyes, only the one called Scara was questionable.

"You see Freya. He is already suspicious; is it not best he, learn the truth from us?" Pohla persisted.

"All right, Pohla. Go ahead," Freya conceded. "This could be a good gage of how we might be received by men folk."

"So, tell me your deep dark secret." Fordoc looked at Pohla and she nearly lost her nerve.

Pohla steadied her nerves and began. "We are not of pure blood. Our mothers were women of man folk forced to breed with orcs. They were slaves, raped and impregnated to produce a bigger, smarter, stronger orc with the ability to fight in the light of day. Warriors for an evil man's army. We were the rejects, because we were female. So, we were put to work as slaves." Pohla finished.

"If you were lucky." Freya added with a bitter laugh.

Pohla hoped this revelation would not elicit disgust from Fordoc but she should not have worried.

"This is your dark secret then?" Fordoc laughed and her anxiety and tension dissolved.

"We were worried how others would react to us. Back in Chimera, we were scorned, beaten and worse." Freya voiced her concern.

"I cannot speak for everyone but you will generally find more tolerance out here on the frontier. However, there will always be those who will not accept you. I, myself, experienced this but I have also made many friends."

Freya noted he was an eloquent speaker.

By this time, the group's progress had stopped—well, all except Scara who was well in the lead. She had picked up her pace to get away from Fordoc's incessant jabbering.

Unaware of what was going on behind her, Scara suddenly turned around and realized no one was following her. She could not see them and could barely hear them. They had dropped that far behind her, probably due to that loud, annoying halfling. How could someone so small make so much noise, enough to alert anything for miles around.

Scara had always been the most serious of them all and was offended by this breach of protocol. Indignant, she stomped back to rejoin her sisters.

"Are we going to march or talk?" Scara protested. She would never be mistaken for anything but what she was: a half-breed orc. Scara compensated for this by trying to be the most professional. Unlike the others, she tended to take things a bit too seriously, perhaps; some of this could be explained by the orc in her. So, this sudden lack of discipline offended her.

"You are correct, Scara," Freya said. "March or talk—not both. It is too dangerous and I think we should find a good spot to hold up and rest until morning. We will make a fresh start then."

This satisfied Scara. She always preferred a plan of action. Once she had a plan, she was happy. And Freya had been thinking about traveling by daylight ever since they escaped.

ORC HAI!

This looked like as good a time as any to start. Afterall, they needed to fit into the world of men.

"From now on, we will travel by day and rest at night," Freya advised.

"Shall I scout ahead for a suitable campsite, Freya?" Scara asked.

"Yes, thank you, Scara. That is a very good idea but do not get too far ahead," Freya smiled as she granted Scara's request. She knew Scara would be elated for days now, having been given this new responsibility.

"All right everyone, let's get moving and with a little less chatter. Let's save that until we make camp." Freya instructed and they all nodded in acceptance, with the exception of Fordoc.

"Problem, Mister Fordoc?" Freya gave him a stern look.

For his part, Fordoc did not realize he was supposed to nod and really was not sure about this whole keeping quiet thing. Like all his kind, Fordoc liked to talk and had more questions, but clearly Freya awaited an answer.

"Hmm," Freya raised an eyebrow at his delay.

"Oh! Sorry, I still have some questions." Pohla nudged him. "But I am sure they can wait until we are camped."

"A bit of a hard-ass!" Fordoc whispered to Pohla as Freya moved off.

Pohla gave him a glaring rebuke, which shut the normally gregarious Fordoc up.

"Sorry," He whispered even quieter.

"I will cut you some slack this time, Mister Fordoc, because you are a stranger and do not know our ways," Freya rebuked him. "Later, I am sure Pohla will explain how things work while you travel with us."

Fordoc finally nodded in acceptance. With that settled and Scara in the lead, they were once more off.

8

For her part, Scara never felt more alive. She was using senses she never knew she had. Breathing in scents on the wind and sorting through the array of unfamiliar smells. She was so wrapped up in excitement, it never occurred to her that her sisters might be experiencing these same feelings.

Once outside, the noisy, smelly confines of the Chimera compounds, her nose and ears seemed to become more acute. She heard a vast array of new sounds, from the delicate rustle of the leaves on the wind, to the creak of swaying trees and the swish of branches, even the plaintive hoot of an owl.

There was also the garish clicking of crickets performing their nightly mating rituals, to the careful footfalls of her companions—well with the exception of that clumsy lead-footed halfling.

Even the air was fresher and cleaner; with none of the foul, acrid, smoky smells of their former habitation, it carried with it the scent of pine, fir and cedar. There were even traces of deciduous species like alder, oak and cottonwood.

This was truly living, Scara thought as her eyes scanned the twilight darkness for threats and a suitable campsite. She heard the stream long before seeing it. It was a tiny thing but it would be carrying clear and cold water down, coming as it did from high up the mountain.

Now, all she had to do was find a decent piece of shelter and they would have an excellent campsite. Then as if hearing her thoughts, she came across a large rocky outcrop sheltered by a rockslide to one side and a small thicket of alder trees on the other.

The rocks had tumbled down the mountain sometime in the distant past, creating a kind of natural shelter for them. Yes, this would make a truly excellent campsite, close to fresh water and sheltered from prying eyes. Scara stopped to let the others catch up.

"How is this, Freya? There is fresh water close and plenty of firewood!" Scara proudly presented her choice as the others caught up.

Freya gave it a quick look. "Yes, this will do nicely. Good job, Scara. All right then, we will make camp here. Let's get to it!" Freya clapped twice.

Fordoc was dumbfounded by the pace of the activity. It was amazing to him how fast and efficiently the camp was set up. There was no shouting or bickering, just a crisp efficiency while he tried to stay out the way.

With the camp set up, it was time for some rest. Freya promised it would be a long day tomorrow. So, as she began to organize a guard schedule, Scara again volunteered for the first watch.

One item they had managed to commandeer was an hourglass, a rather valuable but delicate item, which Freya carefully unpacked.

ORC HAI!

She had just unpacked it when Scara carefully took the hourglass from her and turned it over. When the sand ran out, she would turn it over again. The sand running out would mark the end of her watch and she would wake Tauna for the next watch.

Scara slipped well away from the firelight so her night vision would be at its best. She expected a quiet watch and was annoyed to find that Pohla and Fordoc insisted on sitting by the fire, talking. After trying not to listen for a while, she swept over in a huff.

"If you two are going to talk all night, I am going to bed. Wake me if or when you decide to call it a night." Scara stomped off to her bedroll.

Pohla and Fordoc looked after her as she stomped off. Pohla just shrugged before they resumed chatting in hushed tones.

Scara had no intention of falling asleep but slipped off into a deep sleep anyway. The sun was just rising when Pohla woke her.

"Whhaa! Why did you not wake me sooner?" Scara protested.

"You said to wake you when we decided to rest. So, we have," Pohla explained still aglow from the best time of her life. "We only need a couple of hours rest before the others wake." She led Fordoc away.

Scara watched them depart then rose, rubbing her eyes. "Fine," she grunted before placing some more wood on the fire. Still disgruntled, she walked over and, with a poke, woke Tauna.

"Your watch." was all she said and went back to her bedroll.

Tauna rose and stretched, then turned over the neglected hourglass, checked the fire and waited for sunrise or the others to rise.

Pohla watched the exchange between Scara and Tauna from her bedroll and shook her head. Poor Tauna. This was typical of Scara. She was a hard worker so long as things went her way. When they did not, she could get quite huffy.

Unfortunately, Tauna tended to catch the backlash from those huffs. There was no complaint from Tauna, however; as far as she was concerned, she had gotten more sleep than she expected to get.

The sun was still well below the peaks but the sky was brightening nicely when the hourglass ran out of sand for the second time. Tauna rose from where she sat, stretched and then crept over to wake Freya. Tauna noticed that, here in the mountains, the sun seemed to take forever to climb above the peaks.

The skies had brightened considerably but it would be near noon or later before it cleared the peaks. At just the barest touch, Freya's eyes opened.

"Freya, it is time. Shall I wake the others?"

"Yes, please do that. Thank you, Tauna."

So, Tauna started with the closest. She nudged Fina who woke with a start. "Time to get up." Tauna said.

Fina's startled exclamation woke Scara but Pohla and the halfling still slumbered side by side. Tauna then stepped over to them and knelt.

"Pohla," She whispered and was surprised when Pohla did not move. So, Tauna was about to repeat herself.

"I am awake, Tauna. Thank you." Pohla spoke up.

ORC HAI!

By this time, everyone except Fordoc was awake and moving about.

"What about the halfling?" Scara queried obviously still a bit put out.

"He has a name." Pohla pointed out.

Scara ignored her and continued. "Are we just going to let him sleep. He was up half the night, blabbing with Pohla!" She protested. "I am not planning on carrying him." She added grumpily.

"That is hardly any way to talk about our guest!" Pohla countered.

Fordoc was awake and had been for a wee while now. He lay there, listening and gathering a feel for his traveling companions.

However, this argument now posed a problem. How long should he fake slumber for they were making enough noise to awaken the dead. Best get it over with and wake or how would ever explain his ability to sleep through such a racket?

"I thought you were on the run? So why such a racket and what is for breakfast?" Fordoc piped up.

This brought the squabble to a complete halt and into the silence that followed, Freya began to laugh. In no time at all, they all began to laugh not knowing why but they had not laughed in such a long time. It was a refreshing release of tension.

Laughing was not encouraged among the slaves. Also, there was little to laugh about. The only laughter back at Chimera was the cruel kind, based on someone else's bad fortune.

Suddenly, out of nowhere, a barrage of crossbow bolts interrupted their frivolity. By some chance miracle, they missed everyone and the sisters immediately scattered for cover.

Freya feared they had dallied too long and made too much noise, alerting their pursuers.

"Damn!" Freya muttered. She was relieved when another barrage did not immediately follow the first. "Can anyone see where that came from?"

Only Fina got an approximate location. "They are up in the rocks over there!" Fina pointed out.

"We cannot stay pinned down here," Freya decided. "Grab what gear you can. We will fire one volley then make a run for it."

This brought another barrage of crossbow bolts to which only Pohla was able to return fire.

"Run, halfling, run!" bellowed a gruff voice. This was followed by another volley of crossbow bolts.

This time, Pohla got off a better shot and there was a curse from up the mountainside. Obviously, Pohla's shot found home.

"Those are dwarves!" Fordoc exclaimed in surprised recognition.

With barely a thought for his own safety, he stepped out into the open and began waving his arms.

"Stop! Stop shooting!" He shouted.

Freya had to tackle Pohla to stop her from rushing out to grab Fordoc and pull him back to safety. She wriggled and squirmed in Freya's grasp until the barrage of crossbow bolts ceased.

ORC HAI!

As the barrage ceased, there stood Fordoc, unscathed. He was all contorted up using his arms and legs to protect vital organs. If not for the circumstances, he looked rather comical. When he realized the firing had stopped, he slowly untwisted.

"Thank you!" He began loudly. "There has been a mistake."

Meanwhile, Freya continued to sit on Pohla who once more began to struggle to get to Fordoc.

"Stop squirming, Pohla. He is fine. You will only make things worse. I do not know what he has in mind but it appears to be working." Freya whispered, urgently trying to calm her.

"Let me see him." Pohla demanded.

Until now, Freya had been literally sitting on Pohla to restrain her, not realizing Pohla could not see Fordoc. "I will let you up if you agree to behave." Freya insisted.

There was a pause while Pohla weighed her options. "Oh, all right! I agree."

9

Fordoc felt a little exposed standing out there in the open and more than a little foolish at his brash decision. He was not sure how many dwarves were up there or how many crossbows might be aimed at him, but at least they had stopped shooting.

The dwarves, on the other hand, meant only to chase off these intruders. Orin, their leader, and his six partners, mostly kin, had been test-mining in the area and discovered a very promising vein of ore: a discovery which they were jealously guarding and had no intention of sharing.

Dwarves were short fellows with gruff personalities and hard features most wore their hair long and sported robust beards. Orin's party was no different. Orin and his fellow dwarves, Norin, Dorin, Nok, Tor, Kand and Nalley, had been merrily digging out ore when sounds echoed up to them. They stopped what they were doing to find out what was making all the noise.

Orin had immediately recognized the halfling. It was the females that puzzled him. They were about the height of a dwarf but not as robustly built and they wore hardened leather armor styled in a design similar to that worn by those foulest of creatures—orc.

Most looked quite human or even halfling-ish, but smelled like orcs. Now that elf arrow that hit and wounded Nok confounded him. No orc could touch anything of elf manufacture. This puzzled him even more but perhaps it was just their armor.

One, however, did appear quite orcish. So, what were these strangers? Orin, like most of his kind, preferred to stick to his own kind and not to mix with others. His knowledge of other races was sadly lacking and this appeared to be a case in point. Wait!

Now the halfling was talking again.

"Thank you! There has been a mistake."

"Yes, there has, halfling. You and your females should be gone." Orin replied.

"You will let us depart? We had not meant to trespass. We thought you wanted to kill us." Fordoc knew dwarves could be very territorial and zealously protective of what they deemed theirs; he guessed the sisters and he must be trespassing.

"If I had wanted you dead, you would already be dead. Norin." Orin signaled to another dwarf, who now stood.

This dwarf was armored in heavy dwarven mail. He wielded an unusual-looking crossbow. He threw it too his shoulder and fired six bolts in quick succession without having to re-cock the crossbow. Each bolt flew true and struck a different tree as he altered his aim.

A startlingly impressive display and the first demonstration that any of them had seen of an automatic crossbow. You

ORC HAI!

would have to be very strong to handle that one as it appeared to buck like a mule.

"Very impressive, indeed. I take your point," Fordoc conceded. "So, my friends and I can just leave?" He double-checked to confirm that point.

"Yes, but be warned—if you come back this way, we will kill you." Orin warned.

"We understand!" Fordoc agreed as Pohla, Freya, Fina, Tauna and lastly Scara came out to join him. They began to collect their gear while Pohla fussed around Fordoc.

"I do not know to whom we owe a debt, sir?" Fordoc yelled back.

"Orin, son of Turin, and you?" The dwarf responded.

"I am Fordoc of Cornerbrook. We are in your debt."

Then Freya stepped forward. "I am Freya. I feel it only right to warn you we encountered a large band of wild orcs a day back in the mountains. We slew their leader: a huge, fat thing, and many of his warriors. The rest ran away. Where they went, we do not know. I just thought you should know."

"We were aware of them but now, with their leader dead, they should be no threat to us. However, we will be on our guard anyway, Farewell!"

They were just about to leave when Pohla turned. "I would like my arrows back, please!" She shouted and there was a gruff laugh from above. "I could have killed two of you if I had wanted." She insisted.

"On your way, missy!" Came a rude reply.

Enraged, Pohla turned and, in rapid succession, split each one of the six crossbow bolts. "I would like my arrows back now!" She shouted.

"Damn!" Came a gruff curse. Then there was a muffled discussion from the dwarves' position before two arrows were tossed down to her.

"Now off with you." Orin shouted.

"A good day to you and farewell, Master Orin." Fordoc waved, turned and joined Pohla in retrieving her arrows.

Freya slid into pace beside Fordoc and Pohla. "You were taking quite a chance there." She addressed them in hushed tones.

"I recognized the voice as that of a dwarf. They could not have been your pursuers." Fordoc explained.

"They could have still been hostile and killed you." Pohla interjected.

Fordoc realized his action had been reckless and brash. "Do not worry; I will not do that again," he whispered earnestly. Trying to clarify his action, he continued, "Dwarves are miners. They must be mining close by and mistook us for claim jumpers. There was just no other reason for them to show themselves."

"Unless they mistook us for orcs!" Freya chastised him. She had to admit, however, that his reasoning was sound even though his actions were foolish and risky.

"Yes, you could have been killed!" Pohla insisted again.

Freya then turned on Pohla. "And you! Do not think you are off the hook? What was that foolish stunt with the arrows? I thought I told you before not to do anything so dangerous again and you agreed. You could have been killed."

They both got the message and knew Freya was upset at the unnecessary risk they had taken.

ORC HAI!

"Sorry, Freya," Pohla apologized contritely, "but they are too valuable." Her voice trailed off under Freya's glare.

"Not as valuable as your life. I will not bury another sister!"

"Yes, I agree with Freya on this." Fordoc piped up.

"You have no room to talk, Mister Fordoc!" Freya glared at him, hoping she had made her point. Freya then paused before patting them both on the back. "Good job. Just do not do it again. Come! The day is still young so let's try and make the best of it." She finished with a smile then set off at a brisk pace to catch up to the others.

Pohla and Fordoc hesitated, confused. They had to nearly run to catch up to the others.

Meanwhile, Scara had set a brisk pace and was far out in front. Freya urged the rest to pick up the pace. She did not want Scara to get too far ahead. It was dangerous to get separated.

The pass they were using to traverse the Ered Chimera mountain range wove up and down in a twisting, often rocky trail. As they climbed, the vegetation became sparse and then as they descended, it once more increased.

The sisters traversed the pass for the next two days. During which they used the time to hone the skills they would need to survive both in the wilderness and in the world of men.

They hunted and trapped small game for fresh meat to supplement their rations, so Tauna got her wish. Even Fordoc contributed: he showed them how to forage spices and other edibles in the wild.

Early into the third day, Scara began to see more and more trees. She suspected they had finally reached the end of the mountain range. A forest loomed ahead and it was no place to be separated from her companions. It would be too easy to get ambushed and killed before she could ever warn her sisters, so she stopped to let the others catch up. While she waited, Scara studied the woods ahead.

This was definitely no pocket of trees. This was a forest of tall conifers pressing up against the mountains as if challenging them for space. Yes, she was sure of it now; they had finally reached the end of the mountain range.

As Freya approached, Scara conveyed this insight.

Freya stopped and took a good look ahead. "Yes, I believe you are right."

The forest ahead was light on low-lying vegetation and clear of most other obstacles beneath the tall conifers. This made visibility good and reduced the chances of any nasty surprises.

Still, there was no point in taking any chances. The encounter with Orin the dwarf and his companions a couple of days ago reminded Freya how quickly things could happen.

By this time the others had all caught up. Freya called for a small break to take an early lunch. It was not much of a meal as meals go but, with the promise of finally putting the mountains and Chimera behind them, morale soared and everyone was raring to press on.

"I believe it is time we stayed closer together!" Freya ordered and they were once more off.

This time, it was at a more reasonable pace with everyone closer together. A few hours later, the trees began to give way and they could see rolling fields of tall yellow grass that swayed back and forth in a light breeze like golden waves on the ocean.

ORC HAI!

In no time at all, they reached the edge of the tall grass but even so it was now late in the afternoon heading rapidly towards evening.

Unless Fordoc was mistaken, there was a north-south road somewhere across these fields. Freya could not see it but Fordoc assured her it was there.

Freya had them pause to get their bearings and see if they could spy this road.

"Are you sure there is a road out there?" Scara queried. She, too, saw nothing.

"Yes! We should find it that way," Fordoc pointed after studying the sun and sky. "It is not heavily trafficked but out here few roads see much traffic," he added.

"And there is a town not far?" Scara still sounded dubious.

"Yes, the town of Anvil should be only a few miles down the road." Fordoc was beginning to feel Scara had a problem with him.

"Oh, Scara, you worry too much." Pohla came to his defense.

"What is the problem? I can see the road from here," Fina interjected. "There is even a wagon moving down it."

Everyone turned to look at Fina and then to the direction of the supposed road. Seeing their disbelief, Fina pointed. "Are you all blind? The road runs there." She waved her hand across the field, indicating a faint line running across it. "And there!" she swung her arm back and pointed to a spot, "is the wagon."

They all concentrated on the spot she indicated and—yes—there was something there.

"How in the world did you see that?" Freya asked her little sister as surprised as the rest.

"Seriously, what do you mean? It is clearly obvious. Did none of you see it?" Fina seemed genuinely surprised that none of the others had spotted what seemed readily apparent to her.

"No, Fina, we did not." Freya responded.

"Sorry." Fina apologized.

They were all so conditioned from life in Chimera that, whenever you were questioned, you would immediately apologize in hopes of avoiding a beating.

"There is no need to be sorry for doing a good job, Fina. We must all try to be a little less subservient." Freya insisted.

"Sorry! We will try harder." Came the reply in near unison from all her sisters and Fordoc quickly stifled a laugh.

"I still cannot see it." Scara muttered.

Fordoc waited patiently before speaking. "Right! Shall we catch that wagon?"

"If we did, would we be able to obtain a ride?" Tauna asked hopefully.

Fordoc looked at his companions, suddenly re-seeing them. "It might be best if you let me approach while you remain hidden. We would not want the driver to think he was being attacked by a pack of orcs."

"But we are not orcs." Pohla protested.

"No, you are not but your attire says otherwise." Fordoc pointed out.

"You make a good point, Fordoc," Freya said. "One I had noted before but perhaps you may be able to assist us. You could do us a great service, if you are agreeable that is." Freya paused then quickly continued. "And I know this is a lot to ask but do you think you can catch a ride on that wagon and take it into town? Then, once there, buy us some proper attire or supplies

ORC HAI!

to alter our appearance? Tauna is an amazing seamstress. She can copy or alter whatever you bring us. We will camp well off the road in that grove of trees and await your return."

They all looked expectantly at Fordoc; none more so than Pohla.

"Of course. Whatever you need," Fordoc readily agreed. "It would be my pleasure—but all this needs money and I have very little." He added and was a little worried they did not understand the need for money or if they even had any.

"We would not expect you to pay, Fordoc." Freya explained.

"We have some money. Right, Freya?" Pohla interrupted happily.

Fordoc was a little surprised and looked to Freya for confirmation. "So, what did you do: rob your master as you left," he joked. "Not much of a master to let himself be robbed by his slaves. A wonder you worry about him coming after you!" He crowed, stopping when he saw their serious looks.

"Sorry. But you have to admit it was very careless of him."

Freya was hesitant to tell him where the money really came from so, for the time being, she let him believe what he chose to believe. She would not lie to him but she would also not correct him either for now anyway.

"Our former master and his minions were evil and cruel men but not stupid. We only managed to collect what supplies you see because his attention was focused on other, more important, matters: the first step in his bid for more power. His army marched out to its first real test well equipped and ready. However, this left Chimera cleared of every available resource he thought they would need. Only in the confusion were we able to make our escape." Freya explained.

"We were his possessions, nothing more, and some possessions you treat better than others." Pohla added. They all thought of poor Uta.

"But that does not change the fact we were his possessions and no one is happy about their possessions being taken away." Freya once more took up the story.

Fordoc finally started to realize just how tough it had been for them. "Sorry. That was thoughtless of me. I think I understand better now." He apologized.

"No need. You could not have known." Freya accepted his apology.

"If anybody hopes to catch that wagon, they best leave soon." Fina interrupted.

This brought them all back to the present. Freya then produced three large purses.

"Here is our fortune. There is thirty-one gold pieces, fifty silver and three-hundred-ten copper pieces." Freya presented to Fordoc. She held back the three small gems and the ring, not out of mistrust but rather in reserve in case of an emergency.

Fordoc was dumfounded: he had not in his wildest imagination expected this much money to work with. He should be able to get lots but the selection in Anvil was limited.

"This is more than enough—I'll do my best—but Anvil is small town. I hope I can get all we need. Now, as Fina pointed out, I must be off if I am going to catch that wagon."

"Good luck and be careful!" Pohla wished him good fortune.

"We will be camped in that grove of trees." Freya shouted pointing to where she meant. He waved in acknowledgement.

10

Fordoc sat by the side of the Great North-South Road, awaiting the wagon. The dirt road was well maintained and obviously used more often than he remembered. He had made excellent time crossing the fields, arriving at the road well in advance and unseen by the wagon's driver.

As Fordoc sat and waited for the wagon, he thought how quickly he had fit in with the sisters—well, with the exception of Scara—and how quickly he was feeling lonely.

A feint wisp of dust told him the wagon was getting closer and he was confident he could obtain a ride. Afterall, he was an amiable fellow and no one feared a lone halfling.

Fordoc considered his hearing to be quite good, so that is why he was so surprised when the wagon trundled into view. He had expected to hear it long before it came into view. This teamster obviously knew his stuff and kept excellent care of his equipment.

Pulled by a team of two heavy draft-horses, the large wagon rolled on four spoke wheels, well-greased to roll silently. The sides of the wagon could be adjusted up or down to accommodate various cargoes by the addition or removal of ribbed planks.

Seated on top of the wagon was a giant bear of a man. His hair was dark and bushy to go along with his beard. He had bright, intelligent eyes that looked out from under heavy bushy brows, scanning the road ahead for signs of trouble.

As he spied a figure at the side of the road, he shifted in his seat. The move was barely perceptible but it would allow better access to the heavy crossbow hidden at his side.

His name was Hugo and his imposing size had always served him well on his teamster job. Few would choose to willingly cross him. As the figure stood, he relaxed. The figure was not even half his height and less than one quarter his size. This could only be one thing: a halfling.

Fordoc climbed to his feet as the wagon approached. He tried to look small and harmless, which was not hard for a halfling. Fordoc was suddenly unsure if the wagon would stop so he began to wave his arms.

Hugo was normally a jovial and good-natured fellow until you crossed him—then you could expect the full weight of his wraith—but he almost laughed out loud at the comical appearance and behavior of this lone halfling.

Hugo had contact with more than one halfling on more than one occasion. He knew them to be gentle, peaceful folk with more desire for food and drink than fighting. These were not treacherous folk, so he decided to rein in his team and see what this little halfling wanted.

"Hello, little master. This is truly the last place I would have expected to see anyone, least of all one of the little, folk!

ORC HAI!

What can I do for you, then?" His voice rumbled out in a deep baritone.

Fordoc had been debating what to say for quite some time. At the sight of this bear of a man with a voice that sounded like it echoed from the depths of the earth, he questioned his whole idea of catching a ride.

"S-sorry, sir." He stammered, flustered when normally he was so gregarious. His face suddenly turned red and he stopped to try to regain his composure.

"Come, come little one. I hasn't got all day," Hugo was beginning to feel sorry for this lone soul. "This is no place to be traveling alone."

Fordoc took this as a cue. "You are correct sir. Unfortunately, circumstances have separated me from my companions and I could use a ride to the next town for supplies and to await word. Perhaps they are already there."

"Ha, ha, ha! A ride to town I can offer you, but as for a town it is not much and I will only be passing by it. Now climb aboard. I could use the company."

The big man reached down to offer a hand, which Fordoc gratefully accepted. With no effort at all, Hugo lifted Fordoc up to the seat beside him.

"By the way, my name is Hugo, teamster extraordinaire. Got a cargo you want delivered, I can get it there." Hugo made his introduction.

Fordoc did not doubt this man's ability or mistake his statement for a boast. "Fordoc of Cornerbrook, in your debt." He made a slight bow.

"Cornerbrook?" The big man mulled that over before calling to his team. "C'mon, Bob; you too, Doug," he jostled their reins to start them on their way. "No, can't say I've been there. Though I think I met someone else from there."

This surprised Fordoc for few of his people went adventuring. Not to mention, there were few enough convoys of wagons in or out of Cornerbrook.

"Really? Who? I know of no one else who went adventuring."

"Well, it was a long time ago mind you; perhaps I am mistaken. Either way, it is good to meet you, master Fordoc." Hugo was not the type to argue a point, so he went back to guiding his team, beginning to hum a tune to himself. The tune sounded strangely familiar to Fordoc, but he was having trouble placing it. Curiosity overcame him before long.

"Hugo? That tune you are humming—it sounds so familiar. Where is it from?"

"It is a very old lullaby from home. Do you like it?"

"Yes, it is quite soothing but it sounds very much like a song from my home." And Fordoc began to whistle it. There was a definite similarity; too much so for it to be a coincidence.

"And this is an old lullaby?" Fordoc asked.

"Yes very, very old." Hugo replied.

Perhaps Hugo had met someone from Cornerbrook and that halfling brought it back and modified his lullaby. Now who was credited with that tune? Fordoc thought hard on it and it suddenly came to him.

"Merabo!" Fordoc announced suddenly remembering.

"Yes, Merabo! That was his name," Hugo agreed.

"I was not aware Merabo had ever ventured away from home. Of course, I did not know him personally. Where did you meet?"

ORC HAI!

"We briefly crossed paths in the big city of Edradour, to the south. I believe he was traveling with a bunch of dwarves."

"Dwarves!" Fordoc was shocked.

"Yup, dwarves. Never did particularly care for dwarves: a tad too unfriendly for my taste. Oh well, to each his own, I always say."

Fordoc was beginning to take a shine to this big fellow. In fact, he was almost the complete opposite of his appearance: he was gentle, kindly and good-natured.

"I apologize for doubting you," Fordoc said. Then a thought came to him: Merabo was really old. "Hugo, Just, how old are you?"

After Fordoc's departure, Freya and her sisters swerved south to make camp in a large grove of trees. Her choice of this location would make it easy for Fordoc to spot when he returned.

As Freya approached the grove, she noted that these trees looked really old and they were an odd mix of deciduous and coniferous. There was oak, elm, poplar and maple, all clumped together with fir, pine and spruce.

A truly odd grove indeed, she thought, and much larger than she had expected. She wondered how and why such a large growth remained untouched in these fields.

Even before entering the grove, Freya experienced an unwelcome feeling and hostility from the trees. No sooner had they entered beyond the outer perimeter of trees when a swarm of feather-bodied bat–like creatures, with long needle shaped noses, swooped down on them. These creatures employed their noses like giant mosquitoes.

"Stirges!" Scara shouted a warning.

Freya and her sisters must have disturbed a nest upon entering the woods, which was unusual because generally stirges were not daylight creatures. Swords flew out of scabbards but Scara was the first to slash and sheer the wing off the nearest stirge.

Unlike the others, Scara had her broadsword already out and at the ready from the moment they entered the woods. The wounded stirge flipped and smashed into the ground almost at her feet, where she quickly dispatched the crippled creature with a single swift thrust, then turned her attention to meet the next threat.

Meanwhile, Freya was busy fending of a pair while Pohla, Tauna and Fina stood back-to-back as seven more circled, searching for a way to attack.

A swish of flapping wings alerted Scara to another threat. Instinctively, she ducked and thrust her broadsword upward then smiled as she was rewarded with her blade striking flesh. The blade had stuck deep into the stirge's head, striking just behind the stinger.

Meanwhile, Freya had managed to hack the wings of one of her attackers and seemed poised to finish off the other. Surprisingly enough, Pohla was next to vanquish a stirge, followed rapidly by Fina and, a second later, Freya got her second. It was Tauna who seemed to be struggling.

Not counting the one troubling Tauna, there were still five more of the pesky creatures flapping about them, but the remaining stirges seemed hesitant to press the attack.

ORC HAI!

Then, just as Tauna managed to slash the wing off her lone attacker, she exposed herself and a pair of the circling stirges dove straight at her exposed side. Tauna immediately realized her mistake, squealed in panic and dropped to the ground.

An even worse mistake, for now she not only made it harder to defend herself she had exposed Pohla and Fina to attack.

Freya and Scara realized the danger at the same time and reacted immediately. Freya used her small buckler shield to bat one of the stirges aside while jamming the other in the face with her broadsword.

Scara simply hacked the one Freya had batted aside in half before skewering another which now dove at Freya.

The remaining pair of stirges veered away, beating a hasty retreat to avoid being killed. Pohla flipped her bow into her hands and managed to bring down one of the pair before it escaped.

"Come on, let's find that nest." Freya shouted leading the way.

Only Pohla and Tauna lagged behind; Pohla to retrieve her arrow, while Tauna was slow getting to her feet. Freya had heard that these creatures, besides their affinity for blood, liked to collect shiny and sparkly objects. She hoped it was true; if not, clearing out the nest would be good practice.

Freya quickly lost the trail. Fortunately, Fina was more observant and took the lead and located the nest in no time at all. Two trees had toppled or been blown over and were resting against another much larger tree, which held them from crashing to the ground. In the crook of these trees, three intertwined branches made an ideal nest.

"Fina, you have the sharpest eye. Pohla, you are the best shot. You two stay down here and cover us. We will go up and flush it out. Pick a tree, you two!" Freya indicated Scara and Tauna.

Scara immediately began to clamber up a tree trunk as did Freya. Tauna looked at the trees and to Freya.

"What's the matter, Tauna?" Freya asked.

The problem was that Tauna was scared of heights. "It is so high and I am not a good climber, Freya." Tauna protested.

"Well then be careful." Freya advised.

"It is not that high!" Scara taunted from well up her tree.

Before Tauna could whine anymore, Fina intervened. "I will do it, Freya. Tauna can keep a watch."

"No, Fina, we need you down here to spot trouble and help Pohla kill it. I realize heights may scare you, Tauna, but you must do this. We must come at the nest from all directions." Freya commanded.

Scara was looking down at Tauna impatiently. "It is easy, Tauna: come on up. You will see."

Given no option, Tauna gave up and began to climb. All the three trees were very old, with thick trunks making the climbing easier than she had expected.

All three sisters made good progress up their respective trees.

Scara was closest to the nest when a movement caught Fina's attention. "There! Fire right there." Fina pointed and Pohla lined up her bow, spotted a movement and fired.

There came a dreadful screech and a series of violent thrashing movements from inside the nest, causing a shower

ORC HAI!

of debris and shiny golden objects to rain down. Fina dashed forward and caught one of them.

Turning it over in her hand, she could hardly believe it, it was a gold coin. It was raining gold coins. The concept took a moment for her to fully comprehend.

"Gold!" Fina shouted. "It is raining gold pieces!" She danced around in excitement.

"Gold?" Tauna queried from up the tree, then started back down.

Freya and Scara, however, scrambled up the rest of the way to the nest and lunged inside. There followed a brief commotion with the nest shaking terribly. Suddenly, a stirge flew out and Pohla put an arrow into it before she realized it was already dead.

In point of fact, it was the same stirge she had already killed. Someone had tossed it out of the nest. Tauna picked it up, examined its feathered body closely.

"Look! We got dinner!" She held it up.

Fina looked over dubiously from where she was collecting gold coins. "Are you sure about that, Tauna?"

"If it is food, trust Tauna." Came Freya's voice from overhead.

They all laughed good-naturedly. It was an old joke. You could always trust Tauna to find food.

"Gut it, pluck the feathers, a little salt, some pepper, a few spices. Maybe I could find a tuber or two and perhaps some mushrooms. Stuff it, roast it, I bet it will taste-like chicken." Tauna described their potential meal. She almost made their mouths water in expectation.

"Cook two; they're small." Scara volunteered.

Suddenly, more debris and coins showered down on them from above, interrupting their thoughts.

"I think we will sleep up here tonight. It will be safer and we have slept in far worse places," Freya pronounced, sticking her head out. "Actually, with a little work this could be quite cozy."

"But, Freya, I cannot cook up there." Tauna feared her dinner plans were being shattered.

"Do not worry, Tauna; we will only sleep up here. I for one am looking forward to your cooking." Freya noticed Fina gathering the coins. "Fina, how much have you found?"

Fina performed a quick double-check of her count. "Eighty-five gold pieces," She shouted. "These little buggers were busy."

That was more money than any of them had ever seen, although Freya was beginning to suspect how little this was in the world of men.

She scrambled down to collect their loot. As holder of the groups treasure, Freya carefully accepted the gold coins from Fina and placed them in her purse. Well, all except five coins, which she allocated one per sister.

Each in turn opened their purse and the gold coin joined the copper already inside. Freya slid hers into her cleavage for now. She then turned and shouted to Scara, who had not yet come down.

"Scara, catch!" Freya hurled the coin up.

Scara emerged from the nest and caught the coin. "Thanks!" She examined the coin and smiled, for this was personal wealth and a reward for a job well done. None of them were accustomed to having money and it felt good. This

ORC HAI!

money was theirs to spend, unlike the community pool kept by Freya for group essentials.

"All cleaned out up here, Freya," Scara announced. She then proceeded to scamper down from the nest. "Like you said, it is not the fanciest but we have slept in far worse." Scara then grabbed her gear and headed back up the tree.

The rest followed Scara's example and began hauling their gear up to the nest, except for Tauna, who began to unload her cooking pots and utensils. They had killed eleven stirges and Tauna went around and selected two.

"I have selected the best two for dinner!" She shouted up to her sisters.

"Tauna, when are you going to bring you things up here?" Fina asked.

"Well, not for a while. It depends on if you want to eat. We are certainly not going to cook anything up there." Tauna responded.

There was a good-natured laugh from her sisters as they scrambled down the trees.

"Well, if you have got everything out you need, I will take the rest up." Fina volunteered.

"Thanks, Fina. Let me just double check." Tauna gave it a quick once over.

"Yup, it is good to go. Thanks again." And Fina grabbed the pack and skittered back up to the nest.

11

Later, with preparations for the evening meal well underway and the stirges sizzling nicely on spits over the fire under Tauna's care, Freya was beginning to relax. So far, everything had gone so well. It was then that the wind shifted.

"Goblins!" Scara announced with a start, marginally before the others picked up the scent.

Orcs and goblins were old, old rivals. So old a rivalry that it triggered an almost instinctive reaction in them.

Goblins were shorter and smaller than the average orc, standing on average three and a half feet tall. They had a yellowish green hide, flat faces with broad noses, beady red-black eyes, pointed ears and wide mouths with fangs.

"Pohla, get up into the nest and stay out of sight but be ready with your bow. Oh, and toss down our armor and shields." Freya snapped them into action. Freya did not want that elf bow seen just yet.

Pohla scrambled up and into the nest as the others snatched their weapons in preparation for defending themselves. From up in the nest, Pohla began tossing down pieces of armor, helmets and shields.

The first set down was Scara's, followed by Freya's, then Fina's and finally Tauna's. As each set came down, they assisted the owner into her armor. This dramatically sped up the procedure and, in no time at all they were as prepared as they could be. Frankly, Freya was surprised they had so much time. Surely by now the goblins must have realized they were there. Clearly, Freya gave these goblins too much credit.

There was a crashing of bushes heralding their arrival. Eleven lightly-armed and armored goblins, baring an assortment of weapons from hand axes and scimitars to clubs, burst into the clearing.

The goblins hesitated only briefly, taking stock of the situation, presumably sizing up the numbers. Then they charged, shouting war cries and curses extolling the others' defective lineage and what bodily harm they were about to perform on them.

From above, Pohla did not wait for Freya's signal: she unleashed with her bow. Her first arrow flew straight, killing one of their number, who jerked in agony then dropped like a rag doll. A second followed the first and then a third.

So, intent on their hated rivals, the pack of goblins missed the demise of three of their number. Unfortunately, because the nest was so cramped, it slowed Pohla's ability to reload and aim, so she only managed to kill three goblins with her arrows before they were fully engaged with her sisters. Now she could not fire for fear of hitting one of her sisters.

Still outnumbered two to one, the sisters fought bravely, shoulder to shoulder. Pohla found this too hard to watch and do nothing. She felt completely useless so, against Freya's orders, down she scrambled to join the fight and aid her sisters.

ORC HAI!

Freya seemed to be in the most trouble as three goblins had focused on her.

Freya was doing all she could just to fend them off. That was where Pohla headed, unsheathing her short sword.

The three goblins did not see her approach. Pohla picked her prey; she was about to strike when one of his fellows shouted a warning. The warning came too late and, as the goblin turned to defend himself, Pohla's short sword nearly hacked off his arm at the elbow. He screamed in agony and was abruptly silenced with a quick thrust to the face.

Pohla only made one mistake: leaving her arm exposed too long, allowing one of the other goblins to give her arm a nasty slash. If she had been wearing her greaves, it would have deflected the slash but, in her haste to join the fight, she had not put them on.

Pohla shrieked in pain, clutching her arm. Her attack was just the opening Freya needed. Before the goblin could injure Pohla any further, she swung her broadsword, severing the goblin's spine. Freya was now able to turn her full attention on her remaining foe. Outclassed, she cut him down with a vicious slash to the throat, nearly decapitating him.

With the sudden loss of nearly half their number, the remaining goblins' morale waivered. Their hesitancy gave Scara an opening and she rammed her broadsword into the now unprotected belly of a goblin before twisting and pulling it out.

Its dying cry startled the goblin fighting beside him and Scara took full advantage of it. Her broadsword flashed upward, tearing a horrible wound from waist to shoulder.

The wound was extremely painful but not fatal. However, the goblins next move was.

As black blood poured from the wound, he turned in panic to flee and that was his fatal mistake, for Scara hacked him down from behind. His death was all it took for the remainder to break and run.

As the goblins ran, Freya turned to check on Pohla while Tauna went back to see if she could salvage their meal. It was left to Fina and Scara to pursue the fleeing goblins.

Pohla was down on her knees, clutching her right forearm, an expression of agony on her tear-streaked face. Freya could see blood, a lot of blood. This was a serious wound.

"Tauna, Pohla has been hurt bad. Get your sewing kit!" Freya ordered.

"What?" caught unaware and puzzled, Tauna looked up from what she was doing.

"Now, Tauna. It is serious!" Freya commanded.

Tauna jumped up, dropped what she was doing and scrambled up into the nest. It was almost funny to watch how swiftly she could climb when she was not finding a reason to avoid it. She was back down with her sewing kit in no time at all.

In the meantime, Freya had applied a tourniquet to staunch the bleeding. All of them were well-versed in treating wounds: another one of their tasks at Chimera. There were always those in need of stitching up, from wounded slaves, to orcs, half-orcs and, on a rare occasion, a guardsman.

With needle and thread in hand, Freya went to work. She stitched quickly and efficiently, using as small a stitch as she

ORC HAI!

could manage. It was not pretty, and there would be some nasty scarring, but she had stopped most of the bleeding.

Perhaps a healing potion could minimize that and relieve some of the pain. Unfortunately, they had none of that. Healing potions were expensive, hard to acquire and not for slaves, so Pohla was just going to have to deal with the pain for they had nothing to relieve it except some medicinal herbs.

Pohla was not as used to pain as the rest but she was baring up well enough. She had lost a lot of blood and this concerned Freya greatly.

Freya reached into one of her purses and pulled out the three gems, pondering while moving them about in her palm. Perhaps, she thought, these might fetch enough for a healing potion or to pay a healer.

She took another look at Pohla. "I am taking Pohla into town to find someone to tend her wound." She announced.

"You cannot go alone. We will come with you." Fina objected.

"No, you must stay here to meet up with Fordoc when he returns!" Freya ordered.

"Well, Scara and Tauna can do that. You will need help with Pohla. You cannot possibly manage her by yourself." Fina argued.

"Fine! I do not have time to argue." Freya conceded.

Fina rushed forward to help her with Pohla. Tauna caught up with them as they were turning to leave.

"Here, take, the gold. You may need it." She offered.

"Yes, good thinking, Tauna."

After only a short distance, Freya realized just how grateful she was to have accepted Fina's help. Pohla proved to be extremely weak and a handful for both of them. When she finally succumbed to the trauma of her injury and fainted, she nearly fell out of their arms.

They laid Pohla down and quickly rigged up a stretcher to carry her by using two poles and rope lashed between them to support her. This cumbersome-looking arrangement worked remarkably well. Another trick they had learned back in Chimera. It was often necessary to move the wounded and dead.

With this crude stretcher, they were able to make good time. Pohla lay quietly most of the way to town. From the road, the town of Anvil appeared quite small: not much bigger than Chimera.

Anvil, like all towns out here in the frontier, was walled—although it was not much of a wall, even by Chimera's standards. From what Freya could see, it looked pretty hastily put together.

The vertically mounted timbers were not lashed firmly together, so there were plenty of gaps. Not enough for a man or orc to squeeze through but certainly not providing the best protection, she thought.

They had arrived at Anvil late into the night and the town gates were closed. The entrance into the town was through a sturdy wooden gatehouse. The gates were closed at this late hour and a guard stood watch on the ramparts.

They must have looked a pathetic sight, Freya thought, for the guard waited until they were nearly at the gate before challenging them. "Halt! State your business!" A gruff older male voice demanded.

"We were attacked and our companion was wounded," Freya announced. "Please, we are in need of a healer."

ORC HAI!

Freya hoped they would be allowed access for they could not have looked less threatening: two scrawny females carrying a third female on a stretcher between them. Sure, they still wore their orcish armor but not their helmets, which Freya had smartly left behind at camp.

Freya heard him address someone out of sight.

"Roth, wake up. I need you to keep watch. I have strangers to check out."

The same voice addressed her as a second figure appeared beside him. "There is a one copper head tax for admittance."

Freya could just make out the crossbow in this new guard's hands. The good news was it was not being aimed at them. The first man disappeared then shortly afterward she heard the scrape of a locking beam being lifted from the gate.

The gate began to swing slowly open and a figure in chainmail armor emerged. He wore a metal helmet and had craggy features with short, dark, well-groomed hair streaked with silver. He wore a green tunic, which was trimmed in either silver or possibly white with the stylized image of a castle gatehouse emblazoned on the front over his chainmail armor. The tunic was not new and had seen many years of service. Gentle, intelligent eyes evaluated them from under heavy brows.

"What are you three doing out here alone?" His eyes skimmed over their weapons and armor then focused on Pohla. "What happened here?" He examined her bandage.

"We were attacked by a band of orc." Freya lied. "Our party killed most of them and drove the others off. Pohla was the only one of us wounded enough to need a healer. This was the closest town, so we brought her here. Our party will continue and we will await word or their return." She included just enough truth in her story to make it convincing. Just then, Pohla moaned and he nodded his head in understanding.

"May we pass?" Freya asked.

"Yes, of course. But first I must collect three coppers from you." He sounded truly apologetic.

"I will have to set Pohla down to reach my purse." Freya pointed out. She moved slowly so as not to startle anyone and because her hands hurt.

While they were setting the stretcher down, the guard spied the elf bow and raised an eyebrow.

"That is a very nice bow. Now, where did you get an elf bow?"

"It is Pohla's bow not mine." Freya explained then handed him the three coppers.

"Very nice indeed. I think I see why you survived an armed orc attack." He expressed his appreciation.

"Yes, we were very lucky. Now, how do we find your healer so we can continue to benefit from her ability?" Freya was getting impatient after traveling so far, not to mention her hands hurt—now that they were in sight of help, it was too much to be delayed.

"It is quite late and she may be asleep. I will take you there. I am Douglas, by the way, at your service." He performed a slight bow.

"I am Freya and this is my sister, Fina. Pohla, you've already met." Freya happily introduced them all and was pleased with how smooth this was finally going.

Douglas escorted them through the gate. There he stopped to close and bar it.

ORC HAI!

"Roth, keep a sharp eye out. I shall return shortly after seeing these women to Varina's." Douglas said. "He is a good lad but you got to keep on him. Right! Let's get you ladies to Varina." He guided them into town and away from the castle.

Anvil's lord resided in a castle at the north end of town. The castle (if that is what you could call it) consisted of a three-story square keep with an outer circuit wall.

The circuit wall was built of stone to about seventeen feet high and then finished with wooden timbers. Only the corner towers were finished in stone.

As Fordoc had implied, as far as towns go Anvil was not much. The majority of the buildings were low, one-story structures and made of whitewashed mud brick, then trimmed with wood. Of course, there were a few built of wood and stone: these were usually two-story structures. Most had painted placards hanging out front to identify their particular line of business.

There was a tailor, a butcher, a tanner, a blacksmith and stable. At this late hour, however, nothing was open. Well, with one exception—the Boar's Head Tavern, which still seemed quite lively.

Just as they passed the tavern, Douglas turned down another street heading towards a low stone building with a squat locking blockhouse on top.

"That is Varina's place ahead. She is our healer. Her lights may be out but she will not mind waking to treat such a serious injury." Douglas explained as they approached.

Freya noted the excellent quality stonework of the building. A true craftsman had designed and built it. The building bore the emblem of the Healer's Guild on a placard hanging over its arched doorway. There were two small arched windows on each side of the door. Currently, wooden shutters were securely closed over each window.

"Wait here and I will announce you." Douglas offered. He then marched smartly up to the door rapping smartly on it.

From the sounds coming from the other side of the door, Freya realized it was much thicker than it looked. A light appeared in the upper blockhouse and, moments later, a light could be made out around the edges of the shutters.

"Who has business at this hour with my mistress?" Came a young voice.

"Oztag, it is Douglas. Some travelers have arrived and one of them is hurt badly." He announced.

"Let them enter, Oztag." Came another, more cultured voice.

"Yes, Mistress."

Freya heard a bolt shift, then another and finally a third before the door slowly swung outward. In the doorway stood a tall, red-haired, fair skinned girl—well, a young woman. She was wrapped in a green robe of fine linen, trimmed in fur. She carried an oil lamp in one hand, while in the other she held a large fancy dagger.

The woman named Oztag eyed them suspiciously. Behind her, a tall full-figured woman with long raven black hair approached. From what Freya could see of the room, the inside was rather spartanly appointed.

The older woman was dressed in a long flowing gown made from the finest quality shimmering white material. One Freya had never seen before and not exactly the attire she expected a healer to wear. Although Freya's experience was rather limited—for the healers back at the compound were more like butchers.

Varina surprised Freya and came right out to meet them where she checked Pohla over right there on the stretcher. Pohla moaned softly as Varina examined the blood-soaked bandage.

"Sssh, little one. It will be all right now." She recited an incantation and touched Pohla's injured arm. Pohla immediately relaxed with a sigh.

"I am Varina. Your friend will be just fine. What is her name?" Varina turned addressing Freya.

"Her name is Pohla." Freya offered.

"Pohla, what a lovely name." Varina commented. "Come let's get Pohla inside. I will finish treating her there."

The room was just as Freya suspected: very spartan. There were three beds with clean linen lining each sidewall. Varina lead them to a clean wooden table slightly offset from the center of the room.

A crystal orb hung above the table. Varina and her assistant, Oztag, carefully slid Pohla from the stretcher onto the table.

"There now, Pohla." She spoke soothingly. "Douglas, would you please close the door? We do not need bugs in here."

"Of course, Varina!" He responded with a slight bow and moved to close and bolt the door.

Varina gave a light tap to the orb and it began to glow. It continued to brighten until the entire room was bathed in a near-daylight level of illumination.

Freya began to worry if they would have enough money to pay this healer. As Varina began to unwrap Pohla's bandage, Freya broached the topic.

"Your pardon, Varina, and forgive me for asking, but we have limited money." Freya's voice trailed off.

"You will pay me what you can, but even if you could not pay, I would never refuse to treat a patient." Varina explained, never stopping the process of unwrapping the soiled bandage.

"It is true," Douglas said. "We are very lucky to have Varina."

"She has lost a lot of blood." Varina continued her diagnosis.

"I used a tourniquet and then stitched her up as best I could." Freya explained.

As the bandage came off, it revealed that the wound had stopped bleeding and looked nearly healed. Far better than Freya had expected. Magic, she thought—amazing!

Freya had never encountered someone as polite and caring as Varina.

"I will have to remove your stitching. It is quite good, by the way. You must have had some practice doing this before."

"Yes. I—we have all done this before." Freya admitted.

"Well, they have to go before I can apply a healing salve. The salve should remove any scarring. I find women prefer no scarring. She will require plenty of rest. In the morning, it may be necessary to apply another healing spell."

The entire time she was treating Pohla, Varina was explaining her actions like she was giving instructions.

Of course, Freya suddenly realized how could she have been that slow! Varina was the teacher and Oztag her pupil not her servant.

ORC HAI!

"Oztag, would you get me a no. 2 healing salve please." While Oztag hurried off to retrieve the healing salve, Varina carefully removed Pohla's stitches; stitches Freya had so carefully applied. A faint trickle of blood followed the removal. A whispered touch from Varina made it vanish.

By this time, Oztag had returned with a small blue glass vial. Varina took it and poured the syrup over the wound. She put on a special leather glove and gently rubbed in the salve. As it vanished, so did the wound.

"It is my own concoction and will remove all trace of scarring, new or old." Varina explained with just a hint of pride. "Now, you must let Pohla rest. You may stay here with her or try to find accommodation and a meal at the tavern. She will be much better in the morning."

"Varina, I must take my leave and get back to Roth at the gate." Douglas made his apology and began to depart.

"Of course. Thank you, Douglas!"

"I would spend the night here. The tavern is no place for young ladies, especially this late at night." Douglas added to Freya and Fina before departing with a bow.

"Let us move Pohla to the middle bed, you may take the beds to each side of her." Varina instructed as they began to unroll their bedrolls.

"But your beds are for patients." Freya began to protest.

"Nonsense. As you can see, we are not very busy." When she saw Freya was about to argue, she added. "If more patients arrive then I may require you to move but, for now, they are yours."

This seemed to satisfy Freya. Now all that was left was to move Pohla. Varina noticed Freya and Fina wince ever so slightly when moving Pohla. "Let me see your hands." She requested.

They were resistant so she snatched one from each of them and it only took a glance to realize what had happened; their hands were blistered from carrying that stretcher contraption.

"Oztag, could you grab my green healing salve please."

Freya tried to refuse but Varina would have none of it. Oztag returned and presented a green vial to Varina.

"Rub this into your hands, both of you." Varina instructed as she poured the salve into their hands. They did as they were told and the pain and blisters vanished.

"Now, I bid you a good night." She touched the orb again and it slowly began to fade out but, before it did, Oztag handed them another lit lamp.

12

After catching a ride with Hugo, Fordoc arrived at the junction to the town of Anvil with plenty of daylight to spare.

"Thank you for your kindness, Hugo." Fordoc said as the big man carefully lowered him down off the wagon.

"My pleasure, master Fordoc. Now you be safe!"

"And the same to you, Hugo." Fordoc replied.

With a wave and a word to his team, Hugo was off. Fordoc stood there, momentarily watching as Hugo continued on his way southward, down the Great North-South Road.

Finally, Fordoc made his way to the wooden gatehouse and the walled town of Anvil. He paid the one copper entry tax a pittance compared to some town taxes. Of course, Anvil was not much of a town as towns go, even out here on the frontier.

After passing through the gatehouse, Fordoc set a furious pace, searching for and purchasing the supplies they would need. Fortunately, Fordoc was well versed at bargaining so he managed to negotiate some really good deals with their limited funds.

He collected an assortment of tunics and hoods in various colors, along with new gloves, belts, boots and cloaks for each of them. Fordoc had even managed to save some of their very limited money.

His room at the tavern was quite reasonable at six copper pieces and the one copper meal was surprisingly good and quite large. Over dinner, he had decided that, in the morning, he was going to have one last look around for any deals he may have missed, then head back.

Fordoc was up with the sun and eager to get underway. His thoughts were clearer this morning so, over breakfast, he remembered Pohla mentioning Tauna was an excellent seamstress. He decided he would pick up some bolts of cloth and a new sewing kit.

At one shop, he had seen some colored paints to brighten their drab armor—at least until they could acquire something more suitable. It was too bad he was unable to afford one sample set of armor.

He hurriedly finished breakfast then set about collecting these last few items. While organizing his haul, he came to the realization that it formed quite a large bundle. Not only heavy but cumbersome and, in the hot sun, it did not sound like a lot of fun to carry.

What could he do about that? He still had a few coins left, not enough for a horse but maybe a pony or a donkey if he bargained well. Even so, it would take a monumental bit of bargaining. He could not look desperate in any way.

He planned to check the stable to see what his options were but, before that, he would have to store these goods somewhere. Lugging that load around would be a dead give-away to his needs.

Perhaps, with all he had purchased, surely one of these shopkeepers would hold onto his stuff while he completed the rest of his business. He asked the clothier Athelred, who was more than happy to oblige.

With that accomplished, he was off to the stables he had seen yesterday. It was located on the east side of town and it consisted of a rickety old wooden barn with a corral that butted up against the perimeter stockade wall. The corral, unlike the barn, was well maintained. The blacksmith's stall sat beside the barn.

Just as he passed the Boar's Head Tavern, someone shouted his name.

Freya and Fina woke refreshed and immediately checked on Pohla. She was looking much better but was still resting peacefully. All signs of her wound were gone so Freya decided to let her sleep.

Varina's house was so quiet that Freya guessed no one was up yet, but she was unsure what to do. She settled on opening one of the shuttered windows for a look and to let in some light but was hesitant to go wandering around outside for the same reason she had sent Fordoc into town. Distracted, she was startled when Varina's apprentice, Oztag, appeared out of nowhere. Freya had not heard her approach.

"My mistress wishes me to examine your companion then offer you a morning meal." Oztag reported quietly and politely.

"Thank you, Oztag, that would be most agreeable." Freya whispered.

As Oztag began to gently and methodically examine Pohla, curiosity got the better of Freya. "If you do not mind me asking, Oztag, how did you move so quietly?"

Freya tried to be tactful but had little experience in these matters.

"Where I was born and raised, women were supposed to be neither seen nor heard. There was a feud and my people were murdered. I had to flee and that ability saved my life. Varina took me in. I owe her my life." Oztag explained without missing a beat in her examination.

Well, that explained a lot. "Your mistress is an amazing woman."

"Yes, I have learned much and hope to learn more. I wish to make her proud." Oztag finished her examination without disturbing or waking Pohla. "Your friend's wounds have healed remarkably well but she will need to rest today to regain her full strength. My mistress prefers natural healing to magical, whenever possible."

"Many thanks to you and your mistress, Oztag." Freya watched the young woman smile.

It was the first time she had seen her smile and it changed her appearance quite dramatically. Oztag was quite beautiful.

"Now, if you would follow me, I will prepare you a morning meal or perhaps you would like to freshen up while I prepare the meal?" When Oztag saw them hesitate, she added, "Do

ORC HAI!

not worry: Pohla should not wake for quite some time. After I feed you, I will prepare a light meal for her."

"Should not one of us stay with Pohla so if she wakes there will be a familiar face there to reassure her?" Fina asked.

"We will only be in the next room and I will leave the door open; if she awakens and cries out, you will hear her." Oztag offered a compromise. "My mistress will be down shortly to check my diagnosis." She looked expectantly at them, awaiting a decision.

"Yes, that will be quite acceptable, Oztag. Thank you." Freya decided.

Just as they turned to follow Oztag, Fina spotted a familiar figure out in the street and she dashed to the door, quickly unlocked and pushed it open and called out to him.

"Fordoc!" She watched as he turned and tried to identify where the hail came from.

Seeing his confusion, Fina stepped out and waved until he spotted her. The startled expression on his face nearly made her laugh. His expression immediately changed when he realized where she was and ran over.

"What has happened?" He stopped in front of her and tried to look past her. By this time, Freya had joined Fina.

"There was trouble after you departed and Pohla was hurt. I thought it better to bring her into town but everything is all right now." Freya assured him.

Unfortunately, all Fordoc heard was Pohla and hurt. "Let me see her!" He insisted.

"Of course, but you must be quiet. She needs her rest." Freya saw his concern and felt maybe just a touch of jealousy.

No one had ever cared for her in that way. They stepped aside to let him pass.

"Thank you." he said as he slipped between them and towards Pohla.

It was only then that Freya realized Oztag was missing. Now where had she gone? Probably tired of waiting for us, Freya thought. Well, I cannot blame her. She followed Fordoc over to Pohla, who was resting peacefully.

Fordoc studied her meticulously. "I see no wound. Where was she hurt?"

"The healer here is amazing; she treated Pohla last night. Pohla had a terrible wound on her right forearm. Right there." Fina pointed to where the wound used to be. Fordoc looked again at Pohla's arm.

"You will not find a scar. My mistress prepares a salve which removes any scarring." Came a voice from behind them.

Fordoc nearly jumped out of his skin at the newcomer's voice.

Freya almost laughed but both Fina and she were caught by surprise at her arrival again.

Oztag carried a big tray of food. Fordoc looked up at the woman, who towered over him.

"I know some of you are probably hungry so I have brought the food to you. I will put it over here." She carefully laid the platter on the table Varina had used to work on Pohla last night. When they did not react or move, she added, "If there is nothing else, I will go and check on my mistress. Do try to be quiet and let Pohla rest." Oztag added as she disappeared the way she had come.

ORC HAI!

"Well!" Fordoc exclaimed, positively perplexed. "Who was that?"

"Ah, that was Oztag. She is Varina's apprentice." Freya explained then saw his confusion and added. "Varina is the master healer here. It was she who treated Pohla."

Perhaps it was the smell of food or maybe their familiar voices. Then again, it may have been both of these things. Oztag had tried to keep them quiet but, in the end, it was useless and the result was Pohla suddenly awakened.

"Hey, what is all the noise about? Is that food I smell?" She protested groggily then spied Fordoc and smiled. "Oh! Hello."

"Hello to you, too." He said as their eyes locked.

"You gave us quite a scare." Freya interjected.

"Sorry," Pohla noticed the strange surroundings. "Where am I?" She tried to grasp this change and what had happened but it was like coming out of a dream.

"We are in Anvil, at the healer's residence." Freya explained quietly.

Suddenly, the haze cleared and Pohla remembered. She jerked her arm up for a look at her wound. "What!" She exclaimed in total disbelief. "Was it all just a terrible dream?"

"No, it was no dream." Freya stated flatly. "You were bleeding so badly; I decided we needed to get you to a healer."

"And we had to carry you the whole way. A long, long way," Fina added with a feigned complaint.

"But I see no trace of any wound or even a scar!" Pohla was still perplexed.

"When we got to town, the gates were barred closed. Freya had to talk to the gate guard to gain us entry. Fortunately, he turned out to be a nice old fellow. He was even kind enough to escort us here to the healer's residence.

Her name is Varina, by the way, and she came out to meet us and gave you a quick check up. Then she cast a healing spell on your arm. I tell you, by this time my hands were so sore, I almost asked her to do the same for me." Fina continued her rambling explanation.

"But there is no trace of a scar." Pohla was still unable to believe it. Afterall, she had never seen magic healing but had seen the quality of the healers at Chimera.

"She has some special salve that she rubbed into your arm and that made all trace of it vanish. Wait until you met her assistant." Fina giggled.

"Her apprentice," Freya corrected. "And that was uncalled for, Fina; she has been nothing but courteous to us."

"Sorry! You do not remember the goblin attack?" Fina rambled on.

"I—" Pohla hesitated. She was still finding the whole experience hard to comprehend. Her memory seemed rather hazy.

"And how did you find us?" Pohla turned her attention back to Fordoc.

"Funny thing that. I was just preparing to leave and happened to be walking past when Fina called out to me. I could not believe it. There was a tense moment when I realized someone was hurt and it was you. But everything is good now." Fordoc smiled.

Then Pohla got a very mischievous look. "What do you think? As good as new?" She lifted her arm up for his inspection. As he carefully touched her forearm, she added. "You know a little scar might have been nice."

ORC HAI!

"No! This is much better." He stammered.

"Should not a warrior have a scar or two." She continued to tease him.

"I think any idiot can get a scar, but a really good warrior does not. Their ability prevents them from being injured." Fordoc defended his premise.

"Don't let Scara hear you say that," Fina advised. "She really wants one."

Fordoc did not know how to respond to this. His perplexed look caused the others to laugh.

Freya was about to weigh in and remind him that even the best can get hurt when another voice intervened.

"Good morning! I see no one has listened to my advice. However, I am glad to see you are feeling better, Pohla."

They all turned to see the statuesque Varina approaching. Behind was her very serious apprentice, the red-headed Oztag. Freya, Fina and Fordoc immediately parted to allow her passage to examine Pohla.

"Yes, yes. You look much better this morning, Pohla." Varina noted with a cursory examination. "You lost a lot of blood, young lady, and were in quite a state last night when you arrived. Your friend's stitching probably saved your life. How are you feeling?"

"Fine, perhaps a little weak but it all seems like a dream."

"Yes, it probably does but that will pass. Now that you are awake, you should eat and rest to regain your strength. All your strength should return by tomorrow and you can leave then. But not before."

"All right." Pohla agreed. "I do not know what to say but thank you so very much." She gave Varina a slight bow of her head.

"It is unnecessary but you are most welcome." Varina gave a slight bow in return. "I will leave you now but please eat; it will speed your recovery. And you are all welcome to spend the night here."

As she turned and started to leave, Freya intercepted her. "Many thanks again, mistress Varina. I hope this will cover the cost of your services." Freya produced three small gems and a ring from her purse and presented them to her.

Varina was about to protest but then could feel the magic in one of them. Her hand drifted back over the ring. It was a fancy, silvery ring mounted with a small white stone, which emitted a pale blue glow.

Yes, she thought, it was the ring! Sensing its magic, she experimentally picked it up. Exactly what kind of magic, she could not be sure but it was not evil magic.

"This is a magic ring. What kind I cannot be sure, for I am no wizard. You have two choices: the first is to put it on and see what happens. A little foolish in my opinion but I can tell you that the ring is not evil. It is, however, of elf design and made of Mithral. This gem is a moonstone and one of their favorites.

The other, and best, option is to wait until you get to a larger town like Haghill many days down the road and have the Wizards' Guild there examine it. They charge a small fee but it is worth it. I can tell you though that this ring is worth a lot of money." Varina gave the ring back to Freya.

ORC HAI!

Picking up the gems, she carefully began to examine them. "This is a garnet worth one-hundred gold pieces, the others are agates worth ten gold pieces each. This is far too much. So, I shall include a pair of healing potions if that is satisfactory," Varina offered.

Freya was completely taken aback by the offer of healing potions, for she had no knowledge of the worth of gemstones and this was far more of a return than she expected.

"Yes, That, would be wonderful! Thank you!"

Varina guessed that Freya had little or no understanding of gemology. "Freya, did you not know the value of these gemstones?" By Freya's reaction, Varina realized she was correct, so she offered some advice. "You will have to learn the value of your treasure. Either that or find someone you can trust. There are plenty of unscrupulous types who would take advantage of your inexperience."

"How do you know whom to trust?" Freya asked.

"On the whole, the merchants here in town are an honest group." Varina advised.

"Yes, Mistress Varina is quite right. I have secured most of what we needed at quite reasonable prices." Fordoc interrupted hearing their conversation. "Too bad our funds are near out. I was getting a good rapport with one of the shopkeepers. Since you are here, I should retrieve our goods. You can have the pick of the selection. I was beginning to worry how I was going to haul it all when you hailed me, but now that you are here, it should be no problem."

"Yes, you do that, Fordoc, and once we have changed, perhaps we can add a few more essentials," Freya added. "And no, Pohla, you must rest."

"What will we use for money?" Fordoc asked.

"Do not worry yourself about that. We have acquired a few more coins." Freya hinted slyly.

Fordoc disappeared to collect all his purchases, returning in no time at all with a large bundle, which he laid down and began to unwrap.

Inside, were ten tunics and hoods in an assortment of colors, five pairs of gloves, high soft leather boots, wool cloaks for warmth. The cloaks were all woven of the same mix of brown, green and tan, designed to blend in with their surroundings. There were also five thick new leather belts to attach equipment too, some paint and a new sewing kit.

Fordoc even had money left over, which he presented to Freya. There were five gold, fifty-five silver and fifty-five copper pieces. With the eighty gold pieces Freya had recently acquired, their new total was eighty-five gold, fifty-five silver and fifty-five copper pieces. More than they had before Fordoc left for town.

Fordoc had already selected Pohla's tunic before the others had a chance. She had asked him to find her an emerald one for her before he left. Freya chose sky blue and Fina a maroon. The gloves, boots and belts were all similar—it was just a matter of feel.

Once changed and with their orc armor off, Freya felt more comfortable about venturing out. Freya hoped that they would blend in with these new clothes and without armor. This would be their test for acceptance with regular folk. A benchmark test.

She should not have worried: so far, people barely batted an eye at them. This was, after all, a frontier town and they

ORC HAI!

were used to a very diverse crowd. After a casual stroll around town to get a feel for things, they headed for the shop where Fordoc purchased most of their goods.

"Good to see you again, young master." The shopkeeper greeted them. "Are these fine ladies your traveling companions?" He added with a bow.

"Yes, Athelred. These are two of my traveling companions. This is Freya and her sister Fina." Fordoc introduced them.

"How may I be of service, young mistress?" He addressed Freya, correctly identifying her as the leader.

"You are too kind, sir. We are just weary travelers in need of a few more supplies. After Fordoc left for town, we were attacked by orcs and some equipment was lost. Alas, one of our companions was injured."

"I am so sorry to hear that, mistress. I hope they are all right."

"Oh yes. She is with your healer, Varina."

"Then you have nothing to worry about, mistress. Varina is the best and we are so lucky to have her. Now, whatever I don't have handy, I can obtain. What are your needs?"

"We will need six bedrolls," Freya began.

"Come, come, I have a fine selection to choose from." Athelred led her further into his shop.

And on it went, item by item and, in the end, after a thoroughly interesting and educational tour of his shop, in which Athelred maintained a steady descriptive monologue, Freya settled on six bedrolls, new camping gear (two-man tents, lamps, tinderboxes, flasks of oil, blankets), one-hundred feet of rope, a new tarp (eight by ten feet), a pair of light crossbows for herself and Scara, thirty crossbow bolts, five arrows for Pohla's elf bow, six new packs, three more bolts of linen and—on an impulse—a hardened leather helmet that she intended to give to Scara.

It would also serve as a pattern to modify the bucket-like things they were now using as helmets. Last of all, a donkey that Fina named Jack, for hauling all they had acquired.

Freya considered buying some fresh food and condiments but decided to wait for later, perhaps just before they were to leave Anvil. It was getting on, so Freya settled on a meal, selecting what passed for an inn: the Boar's Head Tavern, where Fordoc had spent the night. The tavern was a small square two-story structure made from local stone and wood. The first floor was the tavern, which served quite a reasonable meal for one copper. The meal consisted of bread, soup, stew and roast meat. On the second floor were rooms for daily rates of six coppers or weekly rates of forty coppers. The Boar's Head was not much for décor but nicer and quieter than Freya and Fina were used to.

Freya selected a table in the corner where they could study the patrons without being bothered. As it turned out, they were barely noticed; even so, Freya planned to leave well before the real evening drinking began.

It was a strange experience for Freya and Fina not to be ordered about, beaten or molested in an establishment not so different from the place they had fled. They were just beginning to enjoy themselves when it became apparent from his fidgeting that Fordoc wished to depart.

"Fordoc, you should go and check on Pohla." Freya suggested.

"No, no, I could not possibly leave you two here unescorted." He countered.

ORC HAI!

"We will be fine. Do not be foolish. Go!" Fina argued.

"Are you sure? I do not know." Fordoc continued to debate as he rose then hesitated.

They could see he was torn.

"Yes, go!" Freya ordered finally.

"Pohla has a true companion there." Fina added to his retreating form.

"Yes, she is lucky." Freya agreed. "We are all lucky now!" Freya continued with a smile to her sister.

The pair of sisters sat a while longer studying the other patrons going about their daily business. The interaction amongst them was not very different to those at Chimera, though far less volatile. So, with dinner finished and darkness not far off, they rose and left. Returning to Varina's, they found Pohla much improved.

Freya rose early the next morning, intending to rejoin Scara and Tauna as quickly as possible. Varina arrived and gave Pohla a final check-up. After a brief examination, she declared Pohla fit enough to travel but advised her not to exert herself.

All were eager to get away, even Jack the donkey seemed impatient to depart. With a fond farewell they were off.

13

Scara had watched as Freya and Fina departed then proceeded to cajole Tauna into assisting her in her plans to improve the camp. The first step was to search for and dispose the goblin bodies.

The search turned up a number of gold and copper pieces but nothing else of any value or use. She located a convenient gully nearby and they proceeded to lug the bodies to the edge of the woods and toss them in the gulley.

"Food for the carrion-eaters." Scara joked as they tossed the last one in.

After dinner and before bed, Scara set about improving the stirge nest but she was interrupted during the process by a pair of stirge trying to gain entry. She killed one and the other flew off.

"Damn!" She shouted. "There must be another nest nearby. Tauna, we will have to wait until morning to track it down. Stirge are night creatures. They should be asleep then."

"But what if they come back tonight?" Tauna protested, a bit worried.

"I will jam something in the doorway. That way, if they try to get in, they will wake us." Scara assured her.

They were not disturbed again that night. The next morning, Scara and Tauna set out to find the nest. This took longer than Scara expected, most of the morning in fact.

As Scara quietly climbed up to the nest, Tauna stood below, crossbow at the ready to kill anything besides Scara that came out. Scara paused just outside the nest, listening intently for any sounds of activity inside.

Hearing nothing, she lunged in, impaling the first stirge she saw before it could awaken. She had believed that, in the close confines of the nest, she would have the advantage and, at first, she did.

Unfortunately, the nest was larger than she expected: there was a second entrance overhead. At present, this nest housed six stirge. She slew a second one a heartbeat after the first; with a slash to its head, she nearly decapitated it.

Then the air was full of flapping wings and pointed noses. All she could do was wildly slash and jab at anything that came near. Just as suddenly, it was over and four stirge lay dead or wriggling on the floor. She quickly dispatched them then heard the twang of a crossbow.

Two stirge had managed to escape out the overhead entrance during the melee and Tauna had been focused on the entrance Scara had used. Like Scara, she had not expected a second entrance.

Caught by surprise, she had to quickly re-aim and fire, surprising herself by hitting one of the pair. As it tumbled to the earth, she quickly reloaded but, by that time, the remaining stirge had vanished. "Got one!" Tauna crowed.

ORC HAI!

"Congratulations!" Scara replied as she tossed one after another of the four stirge she had killed out of the nest. "Keep an eye out; it cannot have gone far."

"Duh! What do you think I am doing down here? I thought you said there was only one way in and out." Tauna protested.

"Well, I guess I was wrong."

"Ho, ho! Scara admits to being—wait—I think—yes, there it is. It is hiding up in the trees." She fired and missed. "Damn, I cannot get a clear shot at it. When I move, it moves."

"Wait a minute. I will grab my bow," Scara emerged from the nest and began to clamber down. This alerted the stirge who moved to avoid this new threat. There was a sharp twang of a crossbow.

"Got it!" Tauna trumpeted success.

Tauna was surprised when it did not fall from the trees. She was sure she had hit it, so why was it flapping against the tree? Then realized what she had done: she had impaled it to the tree with her crossbow bolt. Scara walked over and looked up.

"Nice shot! So, are you going to kill it or leave it up there to die?"

Tauna looked up at it again. "You know, it looks good up there. Why waste another bolt. What do you think?"

"Good choice. Now you are thinking. Hey! Let's go see what the nest holds?" Scara suggested.

So up they scrambled and began rooting around every nook and cranny. They collected a number of gold coins and thought that was all the nest held.

"Look at these!" Scara held out five blue-green gemstones.

Neither knew the value but thought them very pretty so they must be worth something. Satisfied they had found all there was to find, they merrily exited the nest and clambered down, proud of their accomplishments and feeling a bit celebratory. Still, they had nothing but leftovers for dinner.

"Looks like leftover stirge for dinner." Tauna grumbled.

"Not again. I know it tastes like chicken but—" Scara jokingly groaned.

"It is that or rations. Unless you can rustle up something better?" Tauna pointed out.

"How would you feel about goblin?" Scara joked.

"Eeew! I would rather eat my armor." Tauna protested.

"Well at least we have a surprise for Freya." Scara added.

"I hope Freya has a surprise for us, like some real meat." Tauna sighed.

"Me too." Scara agreed.

"Have you noticed there is a shortage of game in here?" Tauna queried Scara.

"Yes, I had," Scara agreed. "Strange."

Back at camp, Scara inspected and surveyed their camp, while Tauna prepared a meal. Satisfied for the moment, she sat down to plot her next move. The nest was well disguised. In fact, they would probably not have seen it unless they were searching for it.

The fire pit was well designed to minimize smoke. However, a screen here, another over there and perhaps a few small pit traps to discourage anyone's prying eyes from using them. Yes, Scara thought, that would do nicely.

With a plan fixed in her mind, she began to search for and collect the materials she needed to build Fortress Scara, as

ORC HAI!

Tauna later dubbed it. In no time flat, Scara had assembled a large collection of tree boughs for poles and stakes.

She sharpened one end of the boughs she selected as poles. The rest she cut into one-foot lengths and sharpened both ends. With her collection of poles and stakes in hand, she wandered a good distance from the camp. Carefully selecting her sites, she rammed the poles into the ground.

Through these she wove rope, a mix of tall grass and brush, effectively creating a screen to block the fire's light from searching eyes. She erected four of these in short order.

Then, to deter anyone or anything from using the screens against them, she set small pit traps and lined them with sharpened wooden stakes. She then began formulating ideas for a quick destruction of the walls. Perhaps with a swinging log or stump. With that thought in mind, she wandered back into camp.

"Yum, yum, stirge again." She announced mostly to herself.

Actually, Scara did not really mind stirge. Back at Chimera, meals tended to be whatever they could scavenge. This had made Tauna a very good cook. She could make just about anything taste good.

Scara's stomach growled as the cooking scents greeted her. "Smells great, Tauna!" She announced as her stomach had already given her hunger away.

Tauna beamed at the compliment. She had re-spiced the stirge and was warming it on a spit over the fire while tubers and wild mushrooms boiled in a pot. There was even an assortment of nuts and berries she had collected. Scara could not identify the nuts and berries but trusted Tauna's instinct when it came to food.

"So? What have you been up to?" Tauna asked, for Scara seemed far too pleased with herself.

"Oh, just a few surprises for any would-be intruders. How much rope do we have?" she asked casually.

"What? Oh no, Scara! Freya will be furious if you use up all our rope and once, she gets back I expect we will be moving on."

"How do we know—"

"Freya would never leave us!" Tauna interrupted defensively.

"It may not be her fault. What if the townsfolk overpower and enslave them. We should be prepared."

"Don't say that. Don't even think it, Scara. Freya will be back." By now, Tauna was frantic and Scara realized she had gone too far.

"Yes, yes, of course you are right, Tauna. I was just being foolish." Scara agreed to placate a visibly upset Tauna.

About noon, Freya, Fina, Pohla and Fordoc left the dusty Great North-South Road and began to trudge overland to their camp in the woods. The tall pale-yellow grass was nearly over their heads, partially obscuring them from view. This did not, however, stop Tauna from spotting them.

Since yesterday's disagreement, Tauna had found the courage to go forth alone, find a tree, climb it and keep watch for her friends. Tauna's heart leapt when she first spotted four figures coming up the road. Then she thought she was mistaken for the donkey confused her.

ORC HAI!

At first, she mistook it for a horse, making the four appear taller. As they neared, her mistake became apparent. It was harder to identify them than she anticipated due to their new clothes.

In the end, it was Pohla and Fordoc she identified. She would have to wait until they were closer to greet them. Only, Fina beat her to the punch spotting her and began waving.

"What are you waving at?" Freya asked Fina.

"Tauna," Fina stated then explained. "She is up there, in that tree."

"You must be mistaken; Tauna is scared of heights." Freya looked to her sister, who continued to point.

In the face of Fina's unwavering commitment, she focused on the spot Fina indicated and, sure enough, there was Tauna waving.

"Sometimes I forget that you have such a good eye, Fina." Freya praised her sister.

No sooner had the two groups reunited and both sides began to regale each other with their exploits as a vast quantity of supplies was laid out for selection.

Scara decided on the midnight blue tunic, while Tauna surprised everyone and selected the scarlet tunic, which she immediately set to altering.

Freya then presented Scara with their first new helmet. Rather than their crude bucket-shaped helmets this new helmet was a round hardened leather cap with a band of iron forming the brim, with a metal nose guard and large cheek guards attached.

Scara was ecstatic. She proudly examined it before trying it on and the effect was instantaneous. It changed her appearance from orc to warrior. Freya smiled, happy with the effect and that she had guessed correctly for it fit Scara perfectly.

Tauna looked slyly up from her sewing. "Freya, we have something to show you, too. Scara, show her what we collected."

This brought Scara out of her reverie. "Yes, yes," she began rifling through her belongings then pulled out a bulging purse. Opening it, she poured out gold and copper coins along with five blue-green gemstones.

"Fifty gold and one-hundred-twenty-four copper pieces plus these beautiful gemstones." Scara and Tauna reeled off the quantity as they tumbled out.

"We had to deal with some more of those pesky stirges," Scara added.

"Very nice, you two," Freya said. "This will boost our reserves." Which Freya quickly calculated at sixty-three gold, twenty-five silver and one-hundred-seventy-six copper pieces.

The gemstones would have to be taken into town to be appraised. Freya had now learned the value of a garnet, an agate and a moonstone: with time she would get this treasure thing figured out and, with new apparel, Freya felt more confident in their acceptance in the world of men.

The day had passed so quickly that, before she realized it, the sun was setting and it was time for dinner. It was here that Freya revealed another little surprise. Before departing town, she had purchased a large cut of beef and she had sworn the others to secrecy keeping it for a surprise until now.

"All I can offer you is roast stirge." Tauna admitted wistfully hoping for an alternative.

ORC HAI!

"I think it is time to celebrate!" Freya presented the roast along with a bag of spices, potatoes, mushrooms and assorted greens to Tauna.

Tauna's eyes were not the only ones that lit up in anticipation and she quickly put aside her sewing and set about preparing the roast for an evening meal. Meanwhile, Fina quickly built the fire and, in no time at all, the roast was sizzling on a spit.

No sooner had the roast begun to sizzle and emit a mouth-watering aroma, when something or someone blundered into one of Scara's pit traps, alerting the sisters, who picked up their weapons.

Well, all except Tauna "Not again!" She cursed, pulling the roast off the fire before grabbing her weapon.

"Pohla, get up into the nest. Fordoc, stick close to me. Now ready your crossbows!" Freya ordered.

The four loaded their light crossbows. Freya had learned from her last encounter with the goblins that it was best to kill as many as you can at a distance. They waited to see what exactly had blundered into their camp this time. Momentarily, it became obvious from the shouts and curses.

"Orcs!" Came their startled responses.

Freya knew, like goblins, orcs always traveled in groups. So, they would more than likely be outnumbered. "Once they break into the open, fire one shot with the crossbows. That should reduce their numbers. Then we charge them." Freya quickly explained her plan. She was not going to wait to lose the advantage of surprise. "Pohla, you will continue to fire from up in the nest and do not come down until I call for you."

Freya was not totally sure if Pohla had heard her, for she had spoken so quietly so as to not alert their intruders. All she could do was hope Pohla had learned her lesson.

But Freya had no time to worry. A large pack of wild orcs, perhaps a dozen or more, in a patchwork of armor and weapons, burst out of the darkness and into the firelight.

"Now!" Freya commanded but she really did not have to.

Four crossbows twanged and their deadly bolts flew and down went four orcs. Pohla and her bow dropped two more in rapid succession. Apparently, Scara and Tauna's work on the nest had given her more room and she was able to fire more freely.

Meanwhile, her sisters had tossed down their crossbows and charged the survivors. Pohla was searching for another target when a huge half-orc in a mix of heavy scale and plate armor emerged into sight, pushing forward another six orc underlings.

On his head was a twin horned iron helmet with nose and cheek guards. She rapidly shifted her aim and, just as he opened his mouth to hurl an insult or issue a command, she fired.

Her arrow entered his mouth and out the back of his neck, severing his spine in the process and silencing anything he was about to say. He toppled over backward, clutching desperately at his throat in agony before hitting the ground with a deafening clatter, his heavy armor no protection whatsoever.

This demoralized his already reluctant reinforcements, who began to scatter in terror. In the mad scramble, Pohla was able to drop another orc with an arrow into his back.

ORC HAI!

She was still trying to get another clear shot at their fleeing forms, when a last orc limped into the firelight and her sights. He must have been the one who had blundered into Scara's pit trap.

By the time he realized his mistake and what was happening, a feathered arrow was sticking out of his chest. He clutched at it hopelessly in agony, then fell face first onto the ground.

All Pohla could think of was, damn, I hope he hasn't broken my arrow. With nothing left to shoot at, she glanced down to see how the fight was progressing and if anyone needed help. She need not have worried for the fight was over.

Her sisters and Fordoc had slain all seven orcs with minimal fuss and had begun rifling through the dead. Well, all except Tauna who had returned to tend to their dinner.

Spying Fordoc, Pohla waved down to him to assure herself he was fine. He looked up, a huge smile crossing his face and he waved back. Freya spied the motion and knew this would bring Pohla down from her excellent observation point.

"Pohla, you stay up there and keep a lookout. Too many of them escaped. I do not want to be surprised if they return with reinforcements."

The expression on Pohla's face told Freya she had been correct. Pohla would obey Freya's command but she was not happy about it. "But Freya, I got their leader." She protested.

"Good for you, Pohla, but all the more reason for you to stay up there. You are our best shot."

When they had finished rummaging through the bodies for valuables, Freya looked at all the dead. "We cannot leave all these lying about here. The smell will attract beasts."

"I know a good place to dispose of them!" Scara volunteered.

Using Jack, Fina and Scara set about removing the bodies from around the camp to keep away the carrion-eaters. This time, the work went much quicker. If Jack minded, he showed no sign of it.

Scara led Jack to the gully she and Tauna had used earlier. There she was surprised to see all the goblin carcasses had vanished. In fact, there was no sign they had ever been there. "I swear we tossed those goblins down here!" Scara pointed to the gully, baffled.

"Oh well, something was hungry." Fina shrugged in dismissal.

"Yeah, but their weapons and armor too?" Scara added stumped.

"Let's not hang around to meet whatever took them." Fina reasoned.

"Agreed."

"We should probably tell Freya." Fina speculated.

"She is your sister." Scara did not want to be part of that conversation.

It took them only one more run and their task was completed, so they returned to camp, where Tauna had dinner nearly ready.

Tauna had been busy and the roast proved every bit as delicious as it smelled. A real treat for them; the sisters seldom were able to scavenge even scraps of beef. Fina was feeling bad for Pohla who was still stuck up in the nest on watch, so she collected her dinner and scooted up to relieve her.

That was the last of the excitement for the night and, with the rising of the sun, Freya had them up and ready for their next adventure. After a quick morning meal, the sisters packed up and were on their way.

With some unexpected extra funds, Freya changed her plans and decided on a quick side trip into the town of Anvil to acquire a couple more of those helmets she had seen yesterday. They had caught her eye but insufficient funds had ruled them out. Now she felt them a worthwhile investment.

14

Later that morning saw Freya and her sisters on the Great North-South Road, bound for the town of Anvil. Jack the donkey was carrying much of their gear thus lightening the loads in their packs, making them less cumbersome. All things considered, this made them a faster traveling party.

They arrived in Anvil at about midday and paid the head tax to enter. Freya knew exactly what she wanted and headed straight to Athelred's shop. She had already decided the helmets would go to Fina and Tauna. They were identical to Scara's and were probably built by the same armorer. The pair cost her sixty gold pieces. Freya would have bought more but that was all Athelred had in stock.

Given time, Freya was confident she could modify hers and Pohla's now that they knew the desired look. They also had a chance to examine a proper set of hardened leather armor. Before leaving town, they stopped for a quick meal at the Boar's Head Tavern before continuing south.

Anvil was pleasant enough but Freya still wanted to put as much distance between them and Chimera as fast as possible.

She was happy with their change of appearance but caught was still caught.

She need not have worried so much, for Kemac and Helene's much vaunted campaign of conquest had gone awry almost before it started. His enemy, Tain of Brogin, had a well-placed spy in their camp. So, Tain was aware of their plans and prepared a nasty surprise for them.

Not long after Kemac's forces had marched out of Chimera a, well-positioned raiding party attacked the undermanned and unprepared compound and citadel. This attack had taken place not long after Freya and her sisters had made their escape.

When Kemac learned his citadel was under attack, he flew into a rage and dispatched a relieving force from his main force, thereby splitting his army—always a bad decision.

The relieving force arrived too late to save his embattled fortress. They found the citadel and compound ablaze. Few there had escaped the slaughter and those that did were taken prisoner.

Not thinking straight, Kemac marched his depleted army right into another ambush, where they were carved to pieces. Kemac and Helene barely escaped, fleeing with a pitifully few followers. Of his surviving orcs and half-orcs, most vanished into the wilds.

With his army defeated and his fortress destroyed, it would be a long time before Kemac and Helene posed any kind of threat to anyone.

For four uneventful days, Freya and her sisters headed south. They stuck to the road during the day, making excellent time, and at night they would camp well off the road. During this time, Freya continued to have them modify their armor to make it look less orcish.

In Anvil, they had all learned how to shape hardened leather and it was amazing what a snip here, a bend there, combined with a little paint could do. Not to mention those new helmets. Freya had them fit the light scale armor to their leather skirts to reinforce them.

Four days out of Anvil saw them nearly halfway to the next town and, so far, they had encountered no other travelers or caravans. Freya was beginning to think they had taken a wrong turn.

Early the next day, Fina spied a group of wagons in the distance. "They are heading our way." She pointed.

No one was more relieved with this news than Freya. "Honestly, Fina. I do not know how you see them. How many are there?" Freya was constantly amazed by her sister's vision.

"Three, no, four wagons, Freya." Fina informed her.

Freya quietly breathed out a sigh of relief. This road and the monotony of the endless rolling fields of tall yellow grass, sporadically interspersed with sparse stands of trees, was starting to get to her.

She refused to call them anything other than stands for there were so pitifully few trees in each. These stands were usually no more than five or six trees and an assortment of brush. Freya and her sisters were unused to this type of desolation, so the sight of these wagons was a welcome change.

At this point, any change to the routine was welcomed. Thinking about how to make contact, Freya decided she would like to time their meeting to coincide with their nights stop.

She hoped these travelers would have some information that they would be willing to share about the next settlement. All she knew so far was its name, Haghill, and that it was supposed to be larger than Anvil, which would not be difficult. She also knew it had a Wizard's Guildhall and an Armorer's Hall.

"Fina, can you spot a good campsite somewhere between us and those wagons? I would like us to meet up with them there."

Fina scanned the way ahead then pointed. "There That looks like a good spot."

"Very good, Fina." Freya patted her on the back.

For the rest of the day, Freya monitored their pace, altering it as needed for she did not want to arrive first. She was taking a chance and guessing the caravans plans but this was the only good campsite around.

Now it appeared she was right. The teamsters had obviously chosen the same campsite and it looked like the caravan would make the campsite first. Everything was working out according to plan, Freya thought. This would be for the best and the more she thought about it, the better it sounded.

The caravan was nearing the campsite and beginning to turn off the road. The wagon master now stood up in the lead wagon, waving his caravan forward, when all hell broke loose.

"Hobgoblins!" Fina shouted.

A hail of arrows descended onto the wagons. Well, to be more precise, the lead wagon. The wagon master toppled off his wagon, bristling with arrows.

That miscue in the ambush saved many a life, allowing the teamsters and their guards the chance to defend themselves as

ORC HAI!

a roar erupted from around the campsite and a large group of hobgoblins swarmed out of the surrounding woods.

Hobgoblins are basically the goblin equivalent of a half-orc and stand six to six-and-a-half feet tall, with dark red-brown hides covered in a short gray-black coarse fur. Like goblins, they have flat faces with broad noses, wide mouths, fangs, pointed ears and red-black eyes.

Freya immediately realized they would have to hurry to save these men or it would be too late. Fortune favored her odds, for the ambush was as poorly planned as it was executed. The hobgoblins should have waited until the caravan was further into the campsite and fired at more than just the lead wagon.

If that was not bad enough, the stupid creatures were obviously too focused on the approaching prize, paying no attention to what approached from the other direction.

"Let's go!" Freya urged. "Pohla, as soon as you can get a clear shot, you stop and take it. Fordoc, you stay with her!" Freya ordered.

On they sprinted. Pohla stopped, loaded an arrow and fired in one motion, while Fordoc stood at her side, readying his sling. Scara was the only one of the sisters who had her crossbow preloaded and ready to fire.

The hobgoblins never saw her coming. Scara fired her crossbow at point blank range into the back of a hobgoblin, who jerked in surprise and died. Before tossing her crossbow down, she thrust her broadsword into the back of another.

Meanwhile, Freya managed to remove the leg of a surprised hobgoblin with her first swipe. His howl as he fell finally alerted his comrades to this new threat. Freya silenced him a moment later while he lay squirming on the ground, then proceeded to dispatch another.

Pohla and her bow had now accounted for a second and third hobgoblin. Even Fordoc managed to drop one.

The surprise and ferocity of this new threat seriously damaged the hobgoblins' morale. Sure, they had inflicted some casualties among the caravan's teamsters but the prize was no closer and now nearly half their number lay dead.

As Freya and Scara killed another hobgoblin each, the remaining hobgoblins' morale dissolved and the only thing this band could think of was survival. En masse, they turned in panic to flee, which provided Fina a clean shot into her opponents back. She rammed her short sword through his spine killing him. She then twisted the sword for maximum damage before removing it.

As the surviving hobgoblins fled, Pohla managed to drop another two. Freya and her party had accounted for thirteen of the twenty or so hobgoblins.

Of the eight teamsters, including the wagon master, four still survived, though all had wounds. The two guardsmen were luckier: they remained unscathed and had dispatched a pair of hobgoblins each.

The senior guardsman and a teamster came over to thank them. It was obvious to anyone with any sense that, without these strangers' timely intervention, they would have been done for. As they approached, Freya stepped forward, removing her helmet to meet them.

"But you are women—" the teamster stammered, aghast at the idea.

ORC HAI!

"Pardon my employer's manners, ma'am," the guardsman interrupted. "Many thanks. We would have been done for without your timely assistance." He bowed.

The teamster was a burly fellow with beady eyes and a large nose. The guardsman stood a head taller than the teamster at a little over 6 feet tall. He was a grizzled veteran with keen intelligent eyes and a sincere demeanor. He wore chainmail under a heavy blue tunic and carried a broadsword and spear.

"My name is Karl and my rude friend here is Garth. We are in your debt."

"My pleasure!" Freya stated.

They were then joined by Pohla and Fordoc. Five women and a halfling, Karl thought, now that was curious. This young one with the halfling was quite attractive. He was trying to figure out who and where they were from when Pohla spoke. She had a strange accent. In fact, they all had strange accents.

"I killed five, perhaps a sixth, and they are still running." She reported proudly.

"That's fine, Pohla, but let's not be rude. Introductions first," Freya turned back to the two men who towered over her.

"My name is Freya, this is Pohla and Fordoc," She indicated the halfling. "Over there is Fina, Tauna and Scara." She pointed each out as she introduced them.

"Pleased to meet you all, and again you have our thanks!" Karl responded.

Karl was baffled by these women and gave them another look. That is when he spotted Pohla's elf bow. An elf bow, he thought, and swords of the finest caliber, perhaps even elf manufacture. He could not tell for sure without a closer look.

Who were these women? Some elf variant, perhaps? That could account for them being alone out here. Elves were known to be a bit of genetic puritans.

"We should get the wagons circled for the night." Garth the teamster finally regained his tongue.

"Yes, you are quite right, Garth," Karl agreed.

"Scara, check out those hobgoblins; make sure they are all dead." Freya ordered.

"With pleasure." Came her reply.

"Can we be of any assistance, Fina and Tauna could have a look at your wounded." Freya offered.

There were realistically only two functioning teamsters, including Garth.

"That is most kind of you." Karl accepted her offer. Fina and Tauna set to attending the two most injured teamsters.

"Have any of you ever operated a team?" Garth queried more than a little doubtful.

These were hardly much of a team: merely a pair of heavy draft horses.

"We can give it a try. Pohla is very good with animals." Freya offered. Her offer was quite reasonable, but she could see the teamster debating the pros and cons in his head.

While he did, Pohla approached one of the horse teams and began to make quick friends with them both, much to Garth's chagrin. Karl gave Garth a condescending look and took charge of the situation.

"Garth, you take the first wagon and lead us in, Tobias, you got the second," Karl turned and looked at Pohla. "Pohla, is it?" She nodded. "The third wagon, if you would."

ORC HAI!

"Now, Freya, you are with me. We will take the fourth wagon. Right, let's move these wagons. Garth! While there is still some daylight!"

The other guardsman, a young freckle-faced fellow, approached and looked at Karl for instructions.

"Gunther, go help Scara clear some of the dead out of the way." Karl instructed as he climbed up onto the wagon then turned and offered Freya a hand up.

She was surprised and pleased by the offer, hesitating only briefly before taking his hand. His strength surprised her as he effortlessly lifted her up into the seat beside him.

"He's a good lad in a fight but you have to lead him around by the nose otherwise." Karl explained.

Freya laughed at his description of young Gunther. Karl smiled and laughed with her. Then something happened to her that had never happened before. She blushed. Surprised, she turned away.

However, Karl was a real gentleman: he stood up and went about his business, pretending not to notice. Instead, he surveyed the other wagons to see if everyone was ready.

Pohla and Fordoc were in the wagon just in front of him, with a loaded donkey tied alongside. The teamster, Tobias, was in front of them, waiting, followed by Garth in the lead, sitting like a lump.

Karl scowled. "Garth, what are you waiting for, an engraved invitation? Get a move on!"

Accustomed to following orders, Garth snapped his reins and cajoled his team to move. He was still cynical about Pohla's ability to handle a team; so much so that once he was moving, he turned around expecting to see problems. Instead, to his surprise, he saw each wagon following without a hitch. In fact, Pohla seemed to be having the least problem.

Garth decided to lead the caravan into a rough semi-circle, thus providing a high degree of protection to those camped inside.

Contrary to Garth's cynicism and in spite of him, the entire process went smoothly. Once completed, the horses needed to be watered and fed. Pohla volunteered to do that and, of course, Fordoc followed. The sisters were very adept by now at setting up a camp. They quickly built a fire and laid out all that they needed.

Scara returned with Gunther in tow. He seemed a little intimidated and awestruck by her, whereas she looked mad.

"Freya, we disposed those hobgoblins and collected all of Pohla's arrows. I even had to finish one off that Pohla only wounded. Found him out there crawling away. His companions just left him to die." Scara's evident contempt in her report. "We located their camp not far from him. What a disgusting dump. They had not been there long. They also had a prisoner at their camp but somebody did not listen to me and let her loose." She glowered at Gunther, who looked thoroughly chastised. "She disappeared into the night like a ghost. Perhaps I can find her in the morning," Scara sighed, shook her head, then continued her report. "I collected fifty-two gold pieces and the same again in copper from the fourteen we killed. The other four bodies had twenty gold and forty copper pieces. There were a few decent arrows and crossbow bolts, some assorted bits of good armor. This gold cup and some silverware."

Freya accepted their portion of the spoils.

ORC HAI!

Scara then handed Karl his portion of the loot before she laid the remainder on the ground to divide up.

Karl was caught totally by surprise at this offer. "No, Freya! You and your companions deserve all the spoils and more. You saved our lives. We would have been done for if you had not intervened." Karl insisted, handing the money back.

With that settled, dinner was soon to follow and Tauna's cooking skills ensured it was a memorable one. None of Karl's party remembered a better meal, on or off the trail and this raised everyone's spirits.

The two seriously wounded teamsters were recovering nicely and resting by the fire, content to be alive and to have full bellies.

15

Sitting around the fire, Gunther's curiosity got the better of him. "Who are you? Are you Amazons?" Gunther blurted.

"Gunther!" Karl gave him a condescending glare. "Don't be rude to the folks who just saved your life. Amazons are a myth," when Freya continued to look at him curious, he explained. "Amazons are females warriors who choose to live separate from men. But they are a myth."

"Yes, I am only recently familiar with that title. I do not think of us as Amazons. Pohla proposed we should call ourselves a sisterhood," Freya tried to explain.

"Sisterhood? The stories say that is what Amazons called themselves." Karl pointed out.

"Oh!" This startled Freya and gave her something to think about.

Karl decided to change the topic of conversation. "Freya, I was curious about your broadsword. May I see it?"

"Of course." Freya said.

Perhaps he could tell her something about her broadsword she thought, as she presented it to him.

Karl examined it with a critical eye. "This is quite a sword. At first, I thought it of elf manufacture. Now I am not so sure. It is of a quality I have not seen before. If you don't mind me asking, where did you get it?"

Freya decided to perpetuate the mystery. "We left our home rather abruptly. We were not welcome or treated well there."

There was an audible guffaw from Fina and Tauna before Freya continued. "We are of mixed race if you had not already guessed and we were treated little better than slaves. So, we collected what we needed in secret and, when the time was right, we fled." Freya had added just enough of the truth to make the story plausible. In fact, without knowing it, Freya had confirmed Karl's own hypothesis. So now Karl was convinced these women were outcast half-breed elves. This would explain why their equipment was so hodgepodge.

With that settled, the evening progressed quite well as they talked of many things. Karl was willing to impart his knowledge of Haghill, among many other matters. He informed Freya that Haghill was another four or five, days' travel south.

Haghill was much larger than Anvil, possessing a proper stone castle and keep with an outer circuit wall surrounding much of the town. The circuit wall was a low eight foot stonewall, topped with a well-built wooden palisade.

More important to Freya was that Haghill possessed both a Wizard's Guild and an Armorer's Hall. She could finally get a proper appraisal of their magic ring and the opportunity to acquire some quality armor.

Karl also gave Freya a quick course on evaluating treasure, during which she got a proper appraisal of her gemstones. It

ORC HAI!

would not make up for experience but it would assist her to better judge a treasure's rough value.

He identified the blue-green gemstones as zircons, worth fifty gold apiece. He weighed and judged the gold cup at probably another fifty gold pieces. He carefully examined the silverware, explaining what to look for, then estimated their value at another forty gold pieces. So, despite its harrowing beginnings, the chance meeting had proven rather illuminating.

Freya and Karl consulted on a guard schedule. The sole exception to the rotation was Scara, who was out trying to lure the escaped female closer with water and food.

The night passed uneventfully and Scara had no luck catching her. Scara hoped that she would have more luck in the morning and capture her for her own good. Unfortunately, with the morning, Scara could still not lure her any closer. The female was frustratingly elusive.

With a hearty farewell, the groups parted ways. Karl and the teamsters headed north while Freya and her sisters headed south. To no one's surprise, Scara chose to take up the rear. This wayward female had gotten under her skin.

Around midday, Fina matched pace with Freya. "We are being followed. It is that woman." Fina reported.

"Are you the only one that has spotted her?" Freya suspected Scara had not given up trying to catch her.

"Scara may have. She is certainly acting odd." Fina speculated.

"I think she has taken this escaped prisoner thing quite personally." Freya ventured.

"You can say that again. That is all she could talk about last night." Tauna said.

"Well, it is understandable. We have all been there." Freya concluded.

That simple statement created a moment of awkward silence as each remembered their treatment and the fate of poor Uta. They could all relate to this poor soul. No clear age had been established but, from Scara's fleeting glances, she was convinced the female was young.

"I think we will stop early today." Freya announced.

"I know, I know: keep a lookout for a good place to make camp." Fina moved forward to take the lead.

"What do you think that was about?" Fordoc asked Pohla.

"I would guess Scara and that prisoner of the hobgoblins." Pohla speculated.

"She cannot be following us!" Fordoc seemed aghast at the thought.

"Scara certainly thinks so and Fina must have seen something." Pohla sighed. "I miss my boys. They could catch her."

"Boys?" Fordoc asked.

"Brutus and Rocky, silly! My hounds from Chimera. I told you about them."

"No!" Fordoc replied.

"Sorry."

No one seemed to notice that Scara was dropping further and further behind. Then, in an instant, Scara veered off the roadway toward a lone tree, a scrawny half dead cottonwood only to return momentarily without her spare water flask.

The sky was clear with few clouds and it was turning quite warm, hot in fact.

Scara reasoned the female would need water and the offering of it another lure to gain some trust and draw her in.

ORC HAI!

As midday headed toward evening, Fina at last spotted a promising rest stop not far ahead.

It looked like a small stand of five or six trees partially surrounded by a thicket of brambles, which should provide a good degree of protection. Freya decided it had potential. In fact, the closer they got the better it looked so Freya called a halt.

The site had obviously been used numerous times in the past by travelers as it provided excellent shelter with fresh water nearby. While the camp was set up, Scara began her sweep of the perimeter for signs of potential trouble and to avoid a repeat of last evening.

"No signs of trouble, Freya. Everything seems quiet out there." Scara reported.

"Very good, Scara." Freya acknowledged then, much quieter for only Scara's ears. "Is she still following us?"

Scara nodded.

"Damn!" Freya whispered, truly concerned.

Once Tauna had the evening meal prepared, Scara collected enough food for two and wandered out into the field, well beyond their camp, in hopes of luring the woman in.

She built a small fire beside a small pond and settled in to wait. Her patience was soon rewarded as a feral face peered at her from amongst some tall grass.

"Hello," Scara said. "Please come join me. It is all right. Everything will be okay. I will not let anyone harm you." Scara spoke in a quiet and reassuring voice while offering food and waving for her to approach.

The young woman emerged, slowly and cautiously, her eyes searching for signs of treachery. She was nearly naked as what was left of her clothes were in tatters. Stopping, she crouched ready to sprint away at the first sign of a trap. Her head and eyes darted from side to side.

Scara could tell this was a young woman, even with the layers of well-embedded dirt and grime. She could also see plenty of cuts and bruises, which needed tending soon as to not become infected. Their number and severity highlighted her mistreatment.

Pretty brown eyes studied Scara then searched again for any signs of a trap. Seeing none, she cautiously moved closer. Scara could tell this young woman was much taller than she or any of her sisters. No clothing they had would fit her; fortunately, they had plenty of cloth and Tauna was a whiz with a needle and thread.

"Please come closer. I will not let anyone harm you. I am the one who rescued you, do you remember?" Scara held out some food. "Here, you must be hungry and cold. Please take some food and join me by the fire."

The young woman dashed forward, grabbing the food and, just as swiftly, she retreated.

"It is all right; you are safe now. Come join me. Those bad creatures cannot harm you anymore." Scara reassured her while remaining relaxed and motionless.

This was difficult for Scara as every bone in her body wanted to leap forward and grab this poor thing, but her restraint seemed to work. The young woman moved closer and, finally, squatted down just across the fire from her.

Scara now patiently studied the young woman while she ate. It was obvious to her this was a fully developed young woman, not an adolescent. Scara slowly and carefully

ORC HAI!

rummaged through her, backpack, all the while being watched suspiciously. Fortunately, Scara found what she was looking for quickly and produced her old cloak with a flourish.

"You look cold. I am afraid none of my clothes will fit you, but perhaps this will help." She handed over the cloak.

The young woman snatched it up greedily and her expression told Scara she had made the right choice.

"My name is Scara," She introduced herself. "What is your name?"

There was the briefest of pauses before she replied. "Scara?" She paused momentarily. "I am Aidelle."

"I am most pleased to meet you, Aidelle."

Aidelle had draped the cloak around her and clutched it to her like a prized possession. Scara let her sit in silence for a while as she was lost in her own thoughts.

"Aidelle," Scara began and the woman looked up. "May I have a look at your wounds, some of them look quite serious." Scara expected some resistance.

"All right." came her subdued reply, which surprised and pleased Scara.

Scara slowly picked up her pack and, as she moved closer, she moved a pot of water closer to the fire to warm. She then withdrew her first aid kit from her pack.

Up close, Aidelle's tattered clothes, the remnants of a dress presumably, looked awful and smelled even worse. These rags would have to go and the sooner the better. Their soiled nature would too readily invite infection.

"These rags will have to go, Aidelle; use my cloak for now. I will get you something better later."

Obediently, Aidelle rose, wincing in pain as she did, and stripped off her rags. Aidelle was slender with pale skin but what Scara found most shocking was the lurid purple blue bruises. She had been beaten remorselessly and probably had a couple of broken ribs.

These injuries would definitely need one of the group's healing potions. Scara wondered how, with all these injuries, Aidelle had managed to keep going, let alone evade her. It must be by sheer force of will alone, Scara reasoned.

Aidelle tightened the cloak around her shoulders and sat back down. She wore no footwear so her feet needed attention first.

"Here, let me have a look at your feet." Scara requested. Taking Aidelle's left leg, she gently lifted it and carefully rested it on her knee for support. "I will try to be gentle but this may still hurt a bit." Scara explained as she began to clean and debride the cuts and lacerations.

Scara worked slowly and methodically, trying to be as careful and painless as possible. What really surprised her was the realization that she and Aidelle had nearly the same size feet. When she finished bandaging Aidelle's foot, Scara pulled out her fur-lined moccasins and tried one of them on Aidelle for size. It fit perfectly.

Scara then cleaned and bandaged the other foot and slid on the other boot. "So how do they feel? Not too tight?"

The expression on Aidelle's face was all the reply she needed.

"They feel wonderful!" Aidelle confirmed. "How did you have my size?"

ORC HAI!

This question caught Scara off guard. She did not know what to say other than the truth. "Um, those are my boots. I noticed your feet were the same size as mine when I was cleaning them. So now we are sisters and as my sister. I wish you to have them."

"We are sisters!" Aidelle responded, ecstatic.

"Of course. We have more in common than you realize. Later, I will tell you, my story. Now, however, I should finish tending to your wounds."

"All right." Aidelle agreed.

Scara began again to clean, debride and stitch, if necessary, any cut, until she had bandaged all of Aidelle's injuries. A little soap and water did wonders but Scara also had two helpers: an alcohol-based disinfectant and a plant extract designed to numb pain. Eventually, all that was left to do was Aidelle's face and hair. So, Scara once more dipped her washcloth in the warm soapy water and began to dab and wipe Aidelle's face and neck. Cleared up, her lightly freckled face was quite pretty.

Once this was accomplished, Scara turned her attention to that unruly mop of hair. Being more concerned with functionality over appearance, Scara kept her hair quite short for ease of maintenance. She only had a brush and shears for grooming.

"Aidelle, do you prefer your hair long or short?"

"Long, if you could, Scara. Please!" Came a plaintive request.

"I will try, Aidelle."

Too bad, Scara thought; short would have made it easier. Oh well. She began to carefully brush Aidelle's hair in an attempt to untangle the mess. She was surprised when it turned out to be easier than she had anticipated—enough that she seldom needed to use the shears. When Scara had finished, she examined her handiwork before applying a snip here and another snip there.

"Much better." Scara smiled and gave Aidelle a light hug. Even this light pressure caused Aidelle to flinch in pain. "I am sorry, Aidelle!" Scara pulled back.

"No, I am fine!" Aidelle tried to reassure her.

"No, you are not! We must do something with those ribs of yours. Do you feel up to meeting my sisters?" Scara knew this would be a scary idea for Aidelle so she was not surprised when Aidelle failed to respond.

"It is all right. We can stay here for now. Earlier, I promised to tell you about me and my sisters. I am no storyteller so bear with me." Scara admitted. Fortunately, the truth of their plight needed no polishing.

When she finished, Aidelle had a better understanding of why Scara had indicated they had much in common. Scara called her companions sisters but none were blood relatives to her. They were as Scara had called them, sisters in misery, and Aidelle would be happy to join them.

Back at camp, Freya had sent Fina up a tree to keep an eye on Scara and her progress because, quite frankly, she was unsure if Scara could pull it off. So, when Scara led the young woman back to camp, she was much relieved. Freya instructed her sisters to be friendly but not overpowering.

As Scara led Aidelle into the camp, she was first greeted by Fina from her lookout position in the tree. "Hi, Scara. I see we have a quest."

"Hello, Fina. This is Aidelle." Scara made the introductions.

ORC HAI!

"Hi." Aidelle replied shyly.

Scara stopped just inside the camp. It was there that Freya approached them.

"I am glad to see you were successful. Welcome!" Freya greeted Scara and then the newcomer.

"Aidelle, this is Freya. She is our leader. Freya, I would like you to meet Aidelle."

Freya raised an eyebrow in surprise. This formal an introduction never came from Scara. What was going on?

"Welcome, Aidelle. It is good to meet you." Freya looked to Scara for an explanation.

Scara merely looked at Aidelle then gave her a light nudge.

Aidelle stood a little straighter and began. "Scara tells me you are the leader so I must ask you. I no longer have any family. They were all slaughtered when the hobgoblins raided our homestead and I was taken away. If you would have me, I would like to join up with you and become part of your family, a sister so to speak." Aidelle knelt, putting her just below eyelevel with Freya, then bowed her head.

So that is it, Freya thought; I should have seen this coming. It was not a big decision and how could she possibly say no. They had readily accepted Fordoc and as a pureblood human, Aidelle should make their acceptance easier.

"You are most welcome to join us, Aidelle." As Aidelle rose Freya reached out to hug her. As she did, Aidelle gasped in pain. "You are injured. Let me see." Freya gently pulled open Aidelle's cloak and examined her bandaged ribs.

"I am pretty sure they are broken." Scara whispered.

"Yes, you are quite right, Scara. Tauna, a healing potion please."

Tauna immediately began digging through Freya's bags, searching for one of two small pewter flasks. Selecting one, she handed it to Freya.

Freya uncapped the flask and handed it to Aidelle. "Drink this. I cannot vouch for its taste but it will help heal you."

Obediently, Aidelle took the offered flask and downed the contents, making a face.

The healing effects were immediate and, to anyone unfamiliar with healing potions, nothing short of miraculous. Her pain disappeared, ribs healed; those lurid purple blue bruises vanished along with most of her assorted cuts and abrasions.

"How do you feel?" Freya asked.

"It's a miracle!" Aidelle stretched, testing her muscles for aches and pains but found none. "Thank you, thank you, thank you!" She hugged everyone who was close.

"Right, let's get those bandages off and I can see if you need any further attention." Freya said.

While they were doing this, Tauna returned with three choices of linen, white, light gray or light brown. "Sorry, we do not have a better selection. Perhaps once we hit town, you can choose something better."

Aidelle looked over her choices and selected the light brown. Without taking a measurement, Tauna set out cutting and stitching.

With Aidelle's bandages removed, Freya carefully examined her for lingering signs of injury. Finding nothing to worry about, Freya wrapped Aidelle in a blanket then Scara placed her cloak back around Aidelle's shoulders before leading her closer to the fire to warm up.

ORC HAI!

During this whole episode, Pohla had kept Fordoc well away to avoid any possibility of an awkward scene. Now, however, she led him over to make their introductions.

"Welcome, Aidelle. I am Pohla and this is Fordoc."

"Thank you. I am most pleased to meet you, Pohla." She then turned to address Fordoc and a strange look crossed her face. "And you too, mister Fordoc."

Pohla knew that look and explained." Fordoc is a halfling."

That got an instant spark of recognition. "Oh, yes. My apologies. I was raised by farming folk with limited knowledge of the world." Suddenly tears came to her eyes and she began to sob, remembering all she had lost and been through. They all crowded around to comfort and support her.

"Hey, before you squeeze the life out of her, I have a tunic for her to try on." Tauna said.

No one other than Aidelle was surprised by how fast Tauna had made it and how well it fit. Tauna had added drawstrings for a more custom fit.

"How?" Aidelle exclaimed. "Tauna, you must be a master seamstress. Even my grandmother, who could really sew, would be astonished!" Aidelle continued as she examined the fit and Tauna beamed at the compliment.

With boots on her feet, a light brown knee-length tunic and Scara's cloak around her shoulders, Aidelle looked much better. Alas, they had no spare armor that would fit her. This would be a priority when they reached Haghill.

All this activity had taken up a lot of time so it was fortunate that Freya had called an early halt to the march even so much of the night had passed. Freya realized this and ordered everyone to get some sleep. Scara collected her bedroll and handed it to Aidelle.

"Here, take, my bedroll, Aidelle. Freya, I will take the first watch," Aidelle was about to protest. "No, you more than any of us need your rest!" Scara commanded.

"All right, Scara." Aidelle conceded.

"I will settle Aidelle in for the night," Freya said. "Wake me next, Scara. Then you can take my bedroll."

With that, everyone settled in for the night. Fina turned and whispered to Tauna. "Lucky you. Looks like Scara has found someone else to boss around."

"Yup! Lucky me." Tauna replied happily.

16

They woke the next morning to an overcast day and the cold damp of rain in the air. They would need to find better shelter than this campsite offered to stay dry. There were no towns nearby, so off they marched, hoping to find cover before the rain started.

"Fina, we need to find some shelter or we are going to get wet, really wet." Freya requested of her sister not long into the march.

Freya had no sooner made her request when the wind began to pick up and the skies continued to darken. This had the look and feel of a real storm. If Fina did not find good shelter soon, things were going to get ugly for them. Everyone watched the route ahead for any sign of shelter, realizing what was coming.

Fina felt the most pressure and was frantically peering into the growing gloom. It was Aidelle, however, who first spotted a potential shelter. Her height probably contributed to why she was first to spy a thatched roof.

She pointed this out to Scara who relayed it to Freya. Caught in an awkward

Dilemma, Freya had to believe Aidelle even though no one else had spotted it.

"Fina, thatched roof!" Freya had to shout to be heard over the wind and was not sure if Fina understood, but pointed in the general direction.

Fina peered in the indicated direction. Seeing nothing, she looked back to Freya as if to say, are you sure? Then only a few steps onward, as she crested a small rise, there it was: a thatched roof.

Fina quickly estimated it to be a two-story structure and, judging by the course of the road, it was located well off of the road. It was definitely their best option for shelter for miles around.

She quickly turned and waved to Freya, indicating she had located the structure. Freya gave her a thumbs up. Well, this was their only option but it was still a good distance off. The fastest way would be to stick to the road then cross overland once they were closer.

Freya signaled everyone to pick up the pace as a light rain began to fall. Just to make matters worse, the wind began to whip up, blowing the rain directly into their faces. So, when Freya directed them to leave the road everyone was glad for, they would not have the rain blowing directly into their faces.

Approaching from the northwest, the structure proved to be a large two-story barn, long since abandoned by all appearances but still in quite reasonable condition. The same could not be said for the only other structure there.

Located not far from the barn were the ruins of what looked to be a large farmhouse. But, as they got closer, it appeared to not be a farmhouse at all but the ruins of a

ORC HAI!

two-story coach house, as Aidelle called it, with the roof and second floor missing.

The coach house was built with a three-foot high stone foundation wall, on top of this whitewashed mud brick rose to the second floor. From there, the second floor was built with wood, judging by the debris scattered around.

To Freya's eye, it looked as if something had just scooped the roof and entire second floor away. Whatever catastrophe struck here, the owners never rebuilt. It was apparent to Freya that this building would provide no shelter. So, the barn it was.

The barn appeared to have fared better than the coach house and was almost unscathed so it should provide adequate dry shelter. By the time they reached the barn, the rain was really coming down.

Like the coach house, the barn was built with a three-foot high stone foundation wall but that is where the similarity stopped. Wood framing and cut timber plank was used for the remainder of the barn.

In the front were two large double doors, flung wide open. They were big enough and more to accommodate a couple of large wagons. Inside, there was even a loft for hay storage.

One of those doors was knocked partially from its hinges and left hanging askew. Freya led them through these doors with weapons at the ready. They formed a semi-circle, expecting and ready for trouble. When nothing happened, there was a brief pause before Freya began to bark orders.

"Fordoc, light a couple of lanterns. Take one and give the other to Aidelle. So far, this looks like a good place to wait out the storm."

It took only a moment for two lanterns to flicker to life, illuminating a good portion of the barn. The barn was far larger than Freya first thought, so she had them methodically search it.

Freya thought it odd that nothing had made a home here. She sent Scara and Fina to scramble up the ladder to the loft, while Pohla covered them with her bow. Again, the search revealed no threats or even signs of occupation among the mounds of hay.

Outside, the barn the wind begun to howl and the rain was pelting down ferociously. Suddenly, a flash of lightning lit up the darkening sky, followed almost immediately by a thunderous boom. It would truly be miserable to be caught out there in the open.

"Let's see if we can close these doors for a bit more shelter!" Freya ordered.

While Freya and the others manhandled the damaged door to close it further, Tauna set out to dig a fire pit.

Working together, they managed to move the damaged door to a nearly closed position, then swung the other door closed and wedged them both into position. Some rope was added to help secure the doors in place. This still left a small gap for wind and rain to enter, but if they were well back, they would hardly notice it.

There was little drywood for a fire but plenty of dried horse dung, which made quite a good fuel for the fire and created an excellent coal for cooking. They had used dried animal dung many times in Chimera as wood was always in short supply.

The bedrolls and extra gear were hauled up into the loft and a small paddock prepared for Jack who seemed happy

ORC HAI!

with this arrangement, especially after hay was tossed down from the loft for him.

While all this was going on, Tauna prepared the evening meal. With no fresh game, she was forced to make a hearty stew with the leftovers. Good thing she was such a good cook.

As the storm raged outside, there was little to do but wait it out. Sheets of lightning danced across the skies, illuminating the darkness, while bolts arced down to strike the ground. These were always followed by a thunderous boom, which shook the barn.

Not long after dinner, as everyone retired to the loft. Scara took the opportunity to begin to train Aidelle. To everyone's surprise, Scara started with the basics of swordsmanship.

Freya had expected Scara would begin with the fundamentals of archery but this was Scara's decision. Bored but not tired, Fina and Tauna remained up to watch Aidelle's first lesson from the loft. They used sticks instead of swords.

At first, Aidelle was hesitant but Scara was determined and displayed far more patience than any of them had ever seen from her. Slowly, bit by bit, Scara's patience began to pay off. It would take more time but Aidelle was showing some promise and her longer reach did give her an advantage.

Evidently satisfied with this first lesson in swordsmanship, Scara patted Aidelle on the back. Scara then switched weapons to show her new friend the basics of a crossbow. After watching a few shots, boredom took hold and even Fina and Tauna settled down for the night.

Scara had Aidelle fire a few more shots until she was satisfied. She then sent Aidelle up into the loft to catch some sleep as she settled in for the first watch.

It was looking to be an uneventful night when, on Pohla's watch, Jack became agitated. Pohla, ever sensitive to an animal's discomfort, went to calm him. It was while tending him she heard orc voices.

Very faint at first and barely audible over the wind, but definitely orc voices. They were arguing and complaining. She heard threats and fighting, then more complaining.

They had to be close. With a last calming stroke to Jack, she bolted back up into the loft. There she quietly woke Freya and explained the situation. Together, they woke the others. They were getting pretty good at readying themselves for a fight quickly and quietly.

Once armed and armored, Freya searched for a good spot to observe what these orcs might be up to. She, was curious for this was not a night to be up and about.

Freya finally found a small crack in the wall and widened it with her knife. Through the crack, she spied at least twelve orcs—perhaps more, it was hard to tell under these conditions. What surprised her more was they were heading for the coach house. The orcs milled about the coach house, complaining, arguing and fighting. Suddenly, there was a brilliant flash of lightning that temporarily blinded her. As her vision returned, the orcs had all disappeared. Freya blinked in surprise.

"They are gone!" She was astonished and she looked again to be sure.

"What do you mean, they are gone?" Scara asked.

"They were right by the coach house. The lightning flashed, blinding me and then, when my vision cleared, they were gone." Freya paused in thought for only a second. "There

ORC HAI!

must be another floor, perhaps a basement or cellar in that coach house."

"Maybe it is the entrance to a subterranean lair or a dungeon." Tauna wistfully speculated.

Eyes rolled. "Oh, Tauna." came a chorus of voices. Then they all laughed.

Scara was the first to turn serious again "How many were there, Freya?"

"I could make out twelve but there could easily have been more." Freya stated.

"So, what are we going to do about them? That is only two to one, odds and we would have surprise." Scara voiced her choice clearly.

"I would hate to charge in there and find out there was a lot more than what I saw." Freya stated the obvious flaw in Scara's proposal. "Anyway, there is nothing to be done until this rain subsides."

"Perhaps we could lure them out and into an ambush." Fordoc suggested.

"Now that is not a bad idea, but what do we use to lure them out?"

Fordoc glanced towards Aidelle.

Scara's reaction was instantaneous. "No! But a fat juicy halfling might work even better!" She glared at him.

Into this awkward moment, Tauna ventured a compromise. "Why not just burn them out?" They all turned to look at her.

"An even better idea, Tauna!" Freya decided.

Pohla pulled Fordoc away as he continued to protest.

"I was not suggesting we stake her out. Just let them see her and they should just charge right out into any ambush we set."

Pohla was desperately trying to shut him up and get him away from Scara. "You know you have to be careful around Scara." She whispered urgently.

When nothing seemed to be working, she got desperate and kissed him. That temporarily ended his protests until she pulled away.

"Wh—bu—"

She kissed him again to raised eyebrows from most of her sisters.

"Come!" Pohla picked up their bedrolls and moving even further away so they could not be heard.

Scara visibly relaxed but still glared at Fordoc's receding back. She even pretended to fire a crossbow bolt at him. "The nerve! Who does he think he is? Aidelle as bait!" She muttered to herself.

Everyone, well everyone except Aidelle, knew to just let Scara work it out and she would calm down. Aidelle, however, was getting visibly agitated and upset at the thought of her newly adopted family perhaps splintering apart.

"Now look at what all this bickering has done. You have upset, Aidelle." Tauna stepped in seeing Aidelle's distress.

This immediately altered Scara from a mother defending her young, to a caring older sister. She moved to put a reassuring arm around Aidelle.

"Sorry, Aidelle. Nothing to worry about. Just a tiny family squabble. It happens all the time." Scara assured Aidelle.

"Yes, Aidelle. Fordoc and Scara squabble all the time." Fina added cheerfully.

ORC HAI!

As Aidelle calmed down she carefully wiped her eyes.

It was at this point that Freya intervened. "There is nothing we can do about our neighbors until the storm passes. I suggest you all try to get some shuteye. When this weather breaks, we are going to be very busy." She carefully avoided any mention of lures or bait. She turned and walked back to her bedroll. One by one, her sisters followed her lead, except for Scara, who had to work off a bit of pent-up emotion.

17

It was well into the morning when the storm finally broke and the sun popped out. The sun's heat quickly raised the temperature and began to dry the ground, evaporating moisture like steam rising from a pot.

The time had come for Freya to announce her intentions. She had thought long and hard about this and had made her decision. There would be no lure to get the orcs to come out. They would simply burn the orcs out. There was plenty of dry hay and horse dung, which would burn quite nicely. To create even more smoke, they had damp green wood. The storm had donated lots of that.

"We are going to barricade the door, start it afire and burn them out," Freya said. "When they try to escape past the smoke and flames, we pick them off."

"Freya, if they are in the cellar there should be a trapdoor access inside the coach house." Aidelle hesitantly interrupted trying to be helpful and pointing out a potential problem she foresaw.

"Are you sure, Aidelle?" Freya asked.

"Well, every cellar I know of has one. We had one at home." she explained.

This added a new dimension to the ambush so Freya quickly modified her plan. "Okay, this might actually work out better. First, we need to locate both doors. We will barricade the cellar door shut with wood and debris, then set the trap door on fire. No orc will want to venture out into the sunlight unless it is forced to and the fire will do that. Those flames should create quite a panic in there and the smoke will help to blind them, making them easy targets. This sunlight should do the rest but we must be quiet or lose the element of surprise. Does everyone understand?" Freya looked at each of her sisters.

Heads nodded in understanding

"Right, let's get to it then." She ordered.

Freya and Fina had no trouble locating the outer cellar door. They barricaded it with branches and debris. They managed to wedge a couple of good tree branches that were broken off in last night's storm up against the door, creating a real obstacle.

It took a little longer to locate the trapdoor in the coach house floor because they had to be careful and search very quietly. If not for Aidelle knowing where best to look, it would have taken far longer.

The floor proved to be quite sturdy and Scara was surprised by how robustly it had been made. Thick and heavy wooden planks were laid over even heavier wooden crossbeams.

Scara waved Freya over upon finding the door and it was obvious that the orcs knew nothing of this door. Together, they

ORC HAI!

carefully cleared the rubble away to expose it and carried over a great pile of hay, horse dung, wood, both lumber and branches.

They started a fire and Aidelle was assigned to tend it. That way, she would be safely away from the fighting as her ability with a weapon was minimal and she had no armor.

Meanwhile, the others selected good firing positions to kill as many orcs as possible as the orcs tried to force their way out of the smoke-filled cellar. Any that survived the barrage and emerged clear of the smoke would be at a great disadvantage in the sunlight, making it easier to cut them down in hand-to-hand combat.

With the trap set, all they had to do was wait for the fire above to do its job and fill the cellar with smoke. As the flames took hold, Freya checked and rechecked her sisters' positions, adjusting them where she saw fit.

Whoever built this coach house intended it to last. The cellar trapdoor was sturdily built: though not as tough as the floor, it was still a challenge to burn through.

As the cellar began to fill with smoke, Freya could hear sounds of commotion coming from inside. Very shortly after that the shouts became curses.

Moments later, the first attempts at opening the door began. These quickly became more frantic and the shouts and curses grew louder. Then someone had the idea to use an axe on the door and the blows came fast and furious.

The fire Aidelle was tending began to burn small holes in the trapdoor, allowing hot coals, burning hay and bits of wood to fall through into the cellar. It began slowly at first but, as the holes expanded, more and more fell through the door, filling the cellar with more smoke and fire.

Whoever was wielding the axe suddenly broke through the door in a shower of splinters and a rush of smoke. He quickly expanded the hole and began batting branches out of the way.

"That damn storm blew some branches against the door, you scum!" Shouted an enormous half-orc. "And the lightning must have started a fire. Next time, I am going to leave a couple of you, useless pieces of filth out here so it doesn't happen again!" He pushed through the door in a cloud of choking smoke.

This was their leader and he carried a large, double-bladed battleaxe, possibly of dwarven origin by the look of it. "You dogs will have to—"

Between the smoke and sunlight, he never saw Pohla's arrows. The first one to the throat silenced him mid-rant: this was followed instantly by a second to the heart, finishing the job. Dropping his axe, he toppled backward into those behind him and that was when absolute chaos erupted.

Adding to this chaos, a large portion of the burning trapdoor collapsed down into the cellar. Aidelle immediately tossed in more hay, causing the fire to flare up.

The terror this created outweighed all other concerns. Fire in its lethally raw form held a primal terror. The stampede this created jammed the door with targets.

Crossbows twanged, releasing their deadly bolts as fast as they could be reloaded. Bodies fell toppling like dominoes, adding to the blockage at the door, their one escape route from the fire. Those behind either pulled the fallen out of the way or clambered over them only to fall to the next bolt or one of Pohla's arrows.

ORC HAI!

Aidelle continued to stoke the fire as fast as she could when the rest of the trapdoor crashed inward, taking the last of the fire with it. Not knowing what else to do, Aidelle frantically began tossing in whatever wood and hay remained.

Two smaller orcs toward the back of the panicked mob spied the possible escape route this created and attempted to clamber out. As the first head appeared, Aidelle tried to push it back down with her wooden pitchfork. The orc merely grabbed her pitchfork and yanked it from her hands, disarming her.

Aidelle backed away and shouted for help as the first orc clambered out followed immediately by a second. Scara and Pohla heard the shout and shifted their aim. Scara's bolt went wild and she tossed her crossbow aside and sprinted to protect her friend.

Pohla, however, did not miss. Her arrow killed the first orc, hitting him in the abdomen before severing its spine as it passed through. The orc spasmed, shrieking in agonizing pain from the elf arrow and collapsed.

This gave the second orc time to defend itself against Pohla's next shot. Crouching, it expertly defended itself with its shield then prepared to face the charging, Scara.

Pohla would not waste an arrow but kept the orc pinned down until Scara reached it.

Back at the cellar door, the reduction of missile fire allowed the handful of remaining orcs to surge free of the congested doorway. Once free of the smoke and congestion, they could maneuver enough to evade or even deflect an approaching crossbow bolt.

The odds were now five to five. The best odds Freya had seen in quite a while. All strategy was forgotten and both sides charged at each other.

Scara approached the last orc as Aidelle backed away to a safer distance, unseen by the orc who was concentrating on Scara. It was only when Scara got closer that she realized her opponent was a female orc or perhaps even a half-orc like herself. Rather than charging straight in, swinging her broadsword, Scara slowed her pace to approach this female more cautiously.

Weaving her broadsword back and forth, Scara sized up her opponent. Her broadsword and its possible origin definitely had the other female orc's attention.

"There is no need for you to die with this scum, sister." Scara addressed her in orcish.

"Sister? I am no sister of yours," She spat back at Scara. "And once I have gutted you, your friend will be my plaything."

The sunlight was obviously interfering with her vision. Scara laughed and whipped off her helmet, revealing her half-orc features.

"Take a good—" Scara began.

"Abomination!" The female orc shouted, lunging at her.

It was a fatal mistake. Spinning, Scara batted aside the orc's scimitar before continuing around her opponent to finish her off with a backhand thrust, severing the spine, narrowly missing the heart and puncturing a lung. She pulled out her sword with a quick twist. The job was done. The female orc spasmed then collapsed backward.

Scara looked down at her. "Such a stupid waste!" She shouted.

ORC HAI!

"AAbbb—" Came a bubbling defiant response before Scara mercy killed her with a quick thrust.

Aidelle had watched the entire exchange and approached Scara, picking up her helmet on the way and handing it to her.

"Not everyone is redeemable." She offered sympathetically.

"Yes—" Was Scara's disgusted response as she donned her helmet. "Come on, let's see how the others are doing."

With eyes still smarting from the acrid smoke, the orcs, emerging from the cellar and into the bright sunlight, had fared no better. They fell like dominoes. Freya's first swing with her broadsword decapitated an orc. She then moved on to assist Pohla and Fordoc, who were her weakest swordsmen.

By that time, Fina and Tauna had slain an orc each and were looking for more. So, when Scara and Aidelle arrived and looked down on the fight from the first floor of the coach house ruins, the fight was over and her sisters were already searching the bodies for loot.

It would be quite some time before they could safely enter the cellar to check it out.

With an acknowledging wave from Freya, Scara led Aidelle back to search the orc bodies for spoils.

Aidelle was hesitant to search the dead but she did after a little encouragement. Scara realized it would never be Aidelle's favorite chore. Between them, they collected some silver and a lot of copper pieces.

Scara deemed none of the orc armor to be big or good enough for Aidelle and, sorting through the limited weapons, she was disgusted by the quality of them and hoped for better from among the other orc dead.

Scara then noted that the fire in the cellar was still burning quite actively so she rolled the two bodies down on top of it, hoping they would smother it.

This action shocked Aidelle. "Scara!" She protested.

"What? We have to put out the fire and they are orc, dead orc at that."

"Yes, I suppose you are right but it just seemed wrong."

"Their corpses are not worth your pity. They would have done far worse to me or you. There is nothing left for us to do here. Come, let's rejoin the others." Scara said, shrugging off the incident.

Upon returning, Scara handed Pohla her arrows. She had no luck finding her crossbow bolt. Aidelle stood to the side and watched in fascination as the spoils were collected and counted.

The big half-orc with the double-bladed battleaxe yielded more money than all the other orcs combined. When the count was done, they had killed eighteen orcs who yielded forty gold, two-hundred silver, one-thousand copper pieces and they had still not searched the cellar.

With funds mounting, Freya decided a reward was in order and handed each three gold, ten silver and fifty copper pieces. To Aidelle, she handed an extra two gold pieces as she had nothing of her own and would need more luxurious things.

This left them with one-hundred-forty-two gold, one-hundred-fifty-five silver and nine-hundred-twelve copper pieces, plus the five gems worth two-hundred-fifty gold pieces in the communal pool. Freya had already earmarked a good portion of the money from the gems to outfit Aidelle.

ORC HAI!

Of the orcs' weapons, they only kept the double-bladed axe: since it was of dwarven manufacture, it was probably re-sellable. From the remaining orc weapons, Scara selected a reasonably good quality scimitar and a pair of excellent quality daggers for Aidelle and presented them to her.

Tauna also had been busy refurbishing a small oval shield with cloth and leather, plus a touch of fur, then a dash of paint. She presented it presented to Aidelle. Aidelle barely knew what to say as tears welled up and she hugged both Tauna and Scara in appreciation.

Because of the late start after the storm, Freya decided that they would camp one more night here then get an early start in the morning. "The roads will be too wet and it is too late to begin traveling. We will spend another night here. I would also like to get a good look inside that cellar." Freya explained.

It seemed that Scara's attempt to smother the fire was working; the volume of smoke had dissipated quite dramatically. As usual, Scara volunteered to enter first.

"Okay Scara, you take the lead," Freya said. She would have liked to enter first but conceded that Scara had the better night vision. "But I will be right behind you. Pohla, you find some good high ground and keep an eye out for any trouble." By trouble she meant more orcs. "No one else follows us unless we call for you."

Aidelle neither wanted nor cared to be part of the cellar search and she knew Scara was unhappy about losing her crossbow bolt, so she thought she might just go have a look for it.

She was also curious about the debris she had spied earlier. While everyone else was distracted, she wandered away. Who knows, she thought, maybe I might get lucky and find that crossbow bolt.

As she approached the debris field, it became obvious it was the remains of the coach house roof and second floor. It was smashed to bits and scattered over a large area.

As Aidelle carefully picked her way through the wreckage she picked up something odd and curious. It looked like a large reddish-black toenail or scale, for lack of a better description.

The scale was roughly twelve by sixteen inches but, beyond that, she had no idea what it was. She elected to keep it and show it to Scara. Aidelle then noticed another, then another amongst the debris. She began collecting them until, in the end, she had collected ten.

Finding nothing else of note, Aidelle headed back. She caught Pohla watching her from atop a wall of the ruined coach house and she waved a greeting.

Meanwhile, the search of the cellar had proved uneventful but potentially very profitable. Freya and Scara found seventy-five gold pieces, five potion flasks and eight gemstones. Freya had no idea of the exact value of the gemstones or the nature of the potions but she was ecstatic about their find.

Scara emerged from the cellar. "Where is Aidelle?" She immediately asked upon exiting and not seeing her with the others.

Fina and Tauna looked around, then at each other, suddenly realizing that Aidelle was missing.

Before Scara could overreact, Pohla piped up. "She went out to look for your crossbow bolt. Do not worry; I am keeping an eye on her. She has found something and is coming back with it now."

ORC HAI!

That got everyone's attention and they clambered up onto the remains of the coach house wall.

"See, here she comes safe and sound." Pohla pointed out.

Yes! There Aidelle was, winding her way back towards the coach house and she was definitely carrying something.

"Why is she carrying animal droppings?" Tauna voiced what most of the others were thinking.

Seeing them all looking at her, Aidelle waved and nearly dropped her collection.

"I do not know what they are but they are definitely not animal droppings." Fina corrected Tauna.

"Sorry Scara," Aidelle said when the others met up with her. "I could not find your crossbow bolt but I found these scattered amongst the debris of the coach house." She then held out her find.

To Freya, they appeared to be scales that glistened a reddish black. She took one and studied it, baffled from what they might have come from.

"Definitely looks like a scale." Scara pronounced.

"So, what do you think they are from?" Aidelle asked Scara.

This stumped her. In fact, it stumped all of them. Not surprising considering the rarity of dragons.

These were dragon scales from the chest or belly of the beast. Dragons shed and re-grow scales as they grow and age. These were probably ready to be shed and were dislodged when the dragon destroyed the coach house.

Unaware of any of this, Freya decided to keep them as a novelty and find out what they were later—perhaps they might prove useful. With nothing left to do, Freya ordered everyone back to the barn.

Along the way, she contemplated another personal cash dispersal. For once again their quantity of coins was growing and she was convinced those eight new gemstones were at least as valuable as the zircons they already possessed, adding another four-hundred gold pieces minimum to their total. That would give them plenty of funds to re-equip.

Little did she know that just one of those gemstones was greater than her entire estimate, a pair of lustrous pale blue stones. These were blue topaz worth one-thousand gold pieces each.

The potions, Freya hoped, would prove useful or at least sellable. She knew they were potions by the markings on the side of the flasks: a lesson she had learned from Karl, and seen at Varina's healing hall.

Things were going so well, it convinced her that a reward was definitely in order. They would all get ten gold, five silver and twenty copper pieces more. She expected this would get everyone excited.

Once they returned to the barn, Freya called them together and told them how proud she was of them, then began dispersing coins. This created a huge buzz of excitement and speculation on what each would buy with their wealth.

Tauna was first to change the subject. "Freya, perhaps Scara and Pohla could locate us some fresh meat for a feast?"

"A good idea, Tauna. Do you two think you can find some game?" Freya asked.

"We can find something but what it will be I cannot guarantee. Can we take Fina too? That should increase our chances?" Scara queried.

ORC HAI!

"Of course. But no stirge; I find they give me gas." Freya joked.

"Right, no stirge." Scara nodded then departed.

Aidelle watched Scara leave then asked. "What is a stirge?"

"Think giant mosquito with fur and bat wings," Tauna explained.

"Eww!" Aidelle shuddered.

"Surprisingly, it actually does taste a little like chicken, believe it or not."

"I will take your word for it." Aidelle replied obviously still revolted at the thought of eating one.

"Now come on, I need those farmgirl eyes of yours to find some fixings like tubers," Tauna grabbed Aidelle by the arm and lead her out the barn. "Wild mushrooms would be nice. Perhaps even some fresh spices."

That left Freya alone with Fordoc, who looked after Pohla. "Relax, Fordoc; she will be fine."

"I know. Scara will not let anything happen to her."

"You are correct there. If you want something to do, go help Tauna and Aidelle collect vegetables. I will keep an eye out for trouble." Freya suggested.

The first to return were Tauna, Aidelle and Fordoc, with a vast array of greens, tubers, potatoes and wild mushrooms.

"They must have had an extensive garden here once. We found all this growing wild now." Tauna reported happily. "Come on! You two you can help me prepare this stuff." She recruited Aidelle and Fordoc.

Scara, Pohla and Fina could not find any big game but they had bagged a pair of pheasants and a large hare.

"Not much out there but we managed to bag these. I think those orcs chased everything else away." Scara displayed their catch.

"Or ate it!" Fina added.

Tauna had plenty to work with for dinner and she did not disappoint. That, and the reward, turned out to be the only excitement for the remainder of the night.

At sunrise, they were all up and raring to be on their way. With money now burning a hole in their purses, they were all anxious to get to town. Haghill, by Freya's calculation, should be no more than four days' travel away.

The morning air was crisp, the sky clear and the pace they set—well, let's just say Freya did not have to cajole anyone along. Most had more money in their purses than they had ever seen and a desire to spend it. The day passed without incident and dinner consisted of a pair of rabbits, courtesy of Pohla's bow.

18

That night, Freya began to wonder (not for the first time) why they called this the Great North-South Road. What was so great about it? There was certainly nothing of interest or much traffic. Perhaps she would get an answer at Haghill.

Another day passed without incident and they camped near a large wooded area. Everything started off quiet but, later into the night, they awoke to the sounds of a fight.

It quickly became clear some goblins were skirmishing with something—well, multiple somethings. None of them could identify what that something or somethings was but it became obvious that it was a lot of somethings. Eventually, Freya decided it was better to investigate now rather than face a new, uncertain threat later.

"Scara, you take the lead!" Freya ordered as they suited up in their armor and fathered weapons.

When they finally came within sight of the skirmish— what a bizarre sight it was! Ahead they saw perhaps fifteen goblins surrounded by at least twice that number of short reptilian humanoids.

The reptilians varied in height from three to three and a half feet tall, with deep rusty-brown scaled hides. On their heads were two smallish horns while red eyes looked out over a crocodile snout.

In their clawed hands, they carried an assortment of weapons from short swords and axes to spears and javelins. Most also carried shields.

Freya noted numerous lizards were already dead and three goblins were down and probably dead.

The goblins were no bigger than the reptiles but wore a variety of armor from hardened leather to a light scale over their yellowish-green hides. Red-black eyes peered out from under iron helmets.

These helmets partially hid their pointed canine-like ears. They were armed similarly to the lizards with short swords, spears and morning stars. The primary difference was that the goblins had short bows.

"Kobolds," Fordoc whispered. "What are they doing here?"

"You know these creatures?" Freya queried.

"I know of them. They live deep underground in the dark recesses, rarely venturing to the surface." Fordoc explained. "These goblins must have raided their settlement."

The kobolds were the ones who made that weird chattering yap they had heard earlier but could not identify. The casualties were quickly mounting on both sides but this did not seem to bother the kobolds.

The goblins, however, would have long since fled if they could. They probably already had but been run down and caught. This was their last stand. A do or die situation and, to Freya, it looked more like die.

ORC HA!

"These kobolds are fierce warriors." Freya noted, a little concerned.

"Not generally. Those goblins must have stolen something very important to them." Fordoc explained.

"I say we let them kill each other and then finish off what's left." Scara suggested.

It made sense. No point in fighting two foes and, the way this fight was going, it would not be going on very much longer.

"Find a good firing position," Freya ordered. "When the last goblin falls, take down the surviving kobolds."

For it was now obvious the goblins were about to lose. There were only two goblins left, compared to ten kobolds. Then, in a flash, it was over: first one goblin fell followed instantly by the other. It happened so fast, it caught Freya and her sisters by surprise.

Then came that odd chattering yap again from the kobolds. Freya could only assume it was some kind of victory cry. The celebration was short-lived as six crossbows and an elf bow unleashed a deadly salvo catching the kobolds completely by surprise.

Half their number fell in that first volley and, as the kobolds turned to face this new threat, the second volley of crossbow bolts and Pohla's third arrow slammed into them. Only one remained standing after that and Pohla dropped him with her fourth arrow.

"Scara, scout for any further signs of pursuit." Freya ordered. "Pohla, keep us covered. Everybody else, search these bodies."

Scara turned to leave and tugged at Aidelle to follow. Freya thought about stopping her but bowed to Scara's wish. Scara knew what she was doing.

"Collect our arrows and crossbow bolts first. I do not want to leave any evidence that we were here!" Freya ordered.

She then had another thought. "Fordoc, see if you can find what these goblins may have stolen to so upset the kobolds." Freya now considered him her resident expert on kobolds, at least the only expert she had.

"Right you are," Fordoc responded before thinking. He realized what he agreed to. "Wait—how am I supposed to do that when I do not even know what I am looking for." He muttered to himself as he moved amongst the corpses searching for anything unusual or out of place.

Just when he was about to give up, he spotted something shiny and green sticking out from a pack under a dead goblin. Rolling the goblin over, he tore open its pack and pulled out a statuette.

It was about twelve inches tall and made of a light green naturally translucent jade. Someone had carved it in the likeness of a woman with kobold features. Small rubies had been inserted for eyes and her arms were raised up over her head as if in offering. Her hands were cupped and she held what looked like an egg. The workmanship was exquisite.

"I found it!" Fordoc announced proud of himself. "These, goblin must have looted a temple or sacred shrine and carried off this image of their deity." He speculated.

Freya interrupted her search and came over to examine his find. "Very good, Fordoc. This is an exceptional piece. Now, how do we return it?"

ORC HAI!

"Return it? Why?" Fordoc looked at her startled.

"I will not invite the potential wrath of a god, any god." Freya announced.

"You have got to be kidding?" He replied.

"No! I am serious, mister Fordoc!" Freya brokered no further discussion.

"Fine." Fordoc submitted to her will but he still thought it that an odd statement for, as far as he had seen, Freya, in fact none of the sisters, had shown any particular level of faith in any deity.

"Return it," He paused, mulling that over. "Perhaps, when Scara returns from scouting, I might have a better idea where to take it." He suggested, stalling for time.

By the time Scara and Aidelle returned, the others had finished searching the bodies and collecting any valuables. They were collecting a staggering number of coins. Thankfully, they had Jack.

"Their route was easy to follow," Scara reported. "There is a steady line of bodies along the way, mostly kobold but a few goblins, and there are arrows everywhere. My guess is the goblins ran out of arrows and that is why they got caught. I counted a dozen more kobold dead to three goblin dead. I—we followed the trail of dead a long way."

"Oh, we also collected sixty gold and four-hundred copper pieces." Scara added and Aidelle then handed over a large bag of coins.

"Did you see anything that looked like the entrance to a cavern?" Fordoc asked hopefully.

Scara gave him a curious look, for their relationship, never great, had been strained since that little misunderstanding with Aidelle.

"Why?" she asked bluntly.

"I found what the fight was about!" Fordoc displayed the jade idol.

Scara whistled. "Very nice. Are we returning it?"

"Yes," Freya confirmed. "At least we'll bring it as far as the entrance to their domain."

"So, was there a cavern entrance?" Fordoc asked again.

"There might have been but the trail led into some really creepy old woods. I did not think it wise to enter as we got a bad feeling from it." Scara explained.

"Yes, yes, that would be perfect. The stories mention an old forest and subterranean caverns." he began to get excited as he relayed what he had heard.

"Good enough for me. Scara, you know the way, lead on!" Freya decided.

Once Freya spotted the woods, she understood why Scara and Aidelle had not entered. The trees indeed appeared old, very old in fact, and there was a sinister feeling and foreboding. These woods were even creepier than the woods they had camped in near Anvil.

"Tauna, light a lantern and give it to Aidelle. Fordoc, hold that statue out in front of you. Aidelle, see if you can use the lamp to illuminate it." Freya instructed.

"A little nervous, sis?" Fina whispered.

"Just hedging our chances. Besides, these woods creep me out." Freya admitted.

"Me too." Fina also admitted.

ORC HAI!

"Me three." Tauna piped up.

They all felt it but, with the illuminated statue, the woods seemed a little less oppressive. They were not far into the woods when Scara suddenly came to a halt.

"The entrance is just up ahead!" Scara announced.

"Fina, Tauna, grab those two goblins we just passed and drag them back here. Scara, you cut some poles. We are going to create a warning marker just outside the tunnel's mouth." Freya instructed.

They all looked at her shocked, well all except Scara.

"What are you waiting for? Snap to it!" Freya ordered.

Freya then led Pohla, Fordoc and Aidelle into the entrance. The cave widened before turning into a proper cavern and then, almost immediately, the path descended.

Freya stopped. "Pohla, you and I are going to build a little pedestal right here."

"Pedestal?" Pohla looked at Freya like she had lost her mind.

"Yes, well, more of an altar of sorts for the Idol." Freya tried to explain.

"Okay?" Pohla nodded, not totally understanding but obeying.

Freya collected and stacked rocks to show Pohla what she meant then used some damp soil as a mortar. From this, Pohla got the idea and joined in, still not totally understanding.

Layer by layer, they built it until Freya and Pohla had erected a roughly two-foot high, pedestal that Freya intended to use for an altar.

Meanwhile, a puzzled Aidelle and Fordoc stood holding the lantern and Idol. Freya was about to have Fordoc place the idol on the altar when an idea struck her.

"Pohla, go see if Tauna has any more of that lion fur, please?"

Pohla gave her a curious questioning look but did as she was asked.

"Um, Freya, this is getting heavy." Fordoc complained. He had been holding the Idol out in front of him all this time.

"Just a little longer. You do not hear Aidelle complaining." Freya added politely.

"That is because she is so polite." Fordoc muttered.

Outside, Scara, Fina and Tauna were putting the finishing touches to their warning marker.

"Tauna, Freya wants to know if we have any of that lion fur left?" Pohla asked.

"What?" Tauna was caught off-guard by the strange request. "Well, yes, a little bit. It is in my pack. What does she need it for?"

"The altar, I think." Pohla tried to explain Freya's plan.

"Altar? What Altar?" Tauna was incredulous.

"Take her the fur and you can see." Pohla advised.

Tauna headed for the cavern while Pohla studied their handiwork.

Each marker consisted of two, two-inch thick tree poles rammed into the ground, forming an X. The dead goblins were tied, spread eagle, across them. It made an impressive warning marker.

"Nice job, Scara!" Pohla said.

"Hey, I helped!" Fina protested.

ORC HAI!

"Yes, it was a team effort." Scara confirmed.

"Still, nice job. It certainly says no goblins wanted."

This completed, Pohla suggested they all rejoin Freya. As they entered, Freya was completing the final preparations in advance of placing the idol. She had draped the fur over the alter, smoothing it down before placing the idol on top.

Freya tested different locations for the lamp to get the best effect. Behind seemed to work best for it made the translucent jade idol appear to glow.

Satisfied, she pulled out a small horn no one had seen her collect and blew into it once, twice and then a third time. They all looked at her, dumbfounded.

Then Fina piped up. "Where did you get that?"

"It was on one of the kobolds I searched. It had to be a signaling device. So, two and two?" She shrugged and they all laughed, all except Scara.

"Are you sure that was the best idea?" She asked.

Before Freya could respond, Fordoc interrupted. "Quiet! I hear something."

As they all quieted, they heard what Fordoc had heard. It took only a couple of seconds to recognize it. Running feet, many running feet.

"Time to go!" Freya ordered leading them back out, leaving the horn behind.

To Freya's horror, the kobolds arrived far faster than anyone could have anticipated. They had not even crossed the small clearing in front of the cavern when they heard a loud commotion. Obviously, the idol had been found.

"Well, I am not going to be run down like those goblins!" Freya decided. She stopped and turned to face whatever came next.

Her sisters followed suit and, just as they did, a large group of kobolds boiled out of the cavern mouth.

Everyone froze.

"No one move," Freya whispered. "Pohla, one arrow into each of the goblins."

Pohla whipped off two arrows one into the head of each goblin. "Now, we bow and try to walk away." Freya instructed.

This was the risky part, Freya thought. She had just turned when suddenly there was a loud commotion behind them. Freya and her sisters spun quickly, expecting the worst. What they saw stunned them.

Eight kobolds emerged from the tunnel, carrying a litter. Seated atop was a female, attired much like the jade idol.

"This has got to be the high priestess." Fordoc whispered in awe.

"We must show some reverence. Everyone, kneel and bow!" Freya ordered.

As Freya watched covertly, the kobolds lowered the litter and the priestess descended from it. She was taller than the males and more human in shape. Surrounded by her bodyguards, she approached the group and paused in front of them. "Leader?" She asked, in reasonable standard.

Freya raised her head. "I am the leader."

The priestess turned to look at her. There was real intelligence in those eyes. "We thank you." She removed a jade amulet from around her neck. "Friends!" She announced and presented it to Freya.

ORC HAI!

She then turned and walked back to her litter without a backward glance. Once she had climbed aboard, the entire party returned the way they had come. There was an audible sigh from the group.

"I thought we were done for, sis! How did you know?" Fina asked.

"Honestly, I was not sure it would work either. We just got lucky." Freya admitted.

"Nonsense. That was brilliant, Freya!" Fordoc crowed.

Freya did not know what to say.

"You have to take more credit for your ability. You stacked everything in our favor."

Freya began to protest, noting how things could have gone awry, but Fordoc ploughed on doggedly.

"And even when the unexpected happened, we came out winners!" Now heads were nodding in agreement.

"He is right, Freya!" Scara spoke for the group.

Unable to argue with the group decision, Freya conceded. "Thanks! Thank you, all."

"And the best part is we don't have to worry about being bothered by any kobolds in the future," Fordoc added. "That trinket will ensure that."

"Yes, quite true, but let us not outstay our welcome." Scara suggested.

The suggestion made sense, so Freya led them in a hasty retreat back to camp where Jack lazed about without a care in the world. It was only once back at camp that Freya finally got the chance to examine the amulet necklace.

It was shaped like a teardrop and made of the same translucent light green jade as the idol. A hole had been bored near the pointed end to accommodate a leather lace. The amulet was just over three inches in length and some odd picture writing was etched deeply into it.

Freya decided the best place for it would be around her neck. That was where the high priestess had worn it so it seemed appropriate.

They got little sleep for the remainder of the night, although some eventually nodded off. This accounted for the late start the next morning. Still, the pace was brisk and the day full of promise.

About midday, they got their first glimpse of Haghill in the distance. The castle and its keep were perched upon a low hill with the town hidden from sight on the south side.

The keep was rectangular in shape and built entirely of large finely cut stone blocks. This was an impressive four-story structure. In fact, the entire castle was built with those same large finely cut stone blocks. Parapets for defense covered the entire castle.

At each corner was a round tower, designed to provide the defenders with maximum firepower while minimizing the risk to the defenders. Additionally, there was an enormous, fortified gatehouse.

In Freya's mind, Haghill made the citadel and settlement at Chimera look like a joke but, in reality, Haghill was just an above average baronial residence.

Freya was alarmed when she realized the entrance to Haghill was further away than she had expected. They could not possibly arrive before nightfall. She also knew from Karl that the gates would close at nightfall and not would not open until the next morning.

ORC HAI!

The baron, a man named Hagar, was not a man to take chances. His great grandfather, Hagrid, had founded the settlement that came to be known as Haghill, short for Hagrid's Hill. The family had ruled here ever since.

Freya waved Fina and Scara over. "I do not think we will make the gates before nightfall." When no one disagreed with her assessment she continued. "That will mean we cannot gain entrance until the morning. So, let's get as close as possible to allow us to enter first thing in the morning."

"Right." They both agreed.

"Do not worry, Freya; I will find us someplace good to camp." Fina reassured her.

The road ahead swung around the base of the hill, under the imposing walls and towers of the castle. It was here as night fell that Fina found an appropriate place to set up camp, under the watchful eyes of the baron's men in the castle.

They were not the first travelers locked out of the town and forced to await the next day after arriving too late, so Fina had no trouble finding a good spot for the night. Freya insisted on posting a guard; even this close to the city, she feared bandits.

The baron, for his part, never left things to chance. Each night, he sent out mounted patrols up and down the road. There were even rangers patrolling outside the castle and town walls.

One such patrol stopped at their camp to check them out. There were six riders in the patrol but only one dismounted and approached to look them over. He was tall, with a sturdy build, blue eyes. On his head was a domed cap.

The cap was made of hardened leather with a wide metal headband wrapping around it while cross straps were added for strength. To this, a large metal teardrop noseguard was attached.

The rider was armored in chainmail, which was partially covered by a red jerkin with black trim. A golden boar's head crest adorned the chest of his jerkin. He carried a large kite-shaped shield and spear. At his side was a long broadsword and on his legs were tall leather riding boots.

Fina was on watch and she immediately woke Freya as soon as she spotted the approaching patrol, long before it arrived. This woke most of the others.

"You in the camp—night constabulary. Just checking to see if you are all right?" The fellow hailed the camp.

"Yes, yes, we are. Thank you for your concern. My name is Freya—" Just then Aidelle approached and whispered into her ear. "There is someone lurking about our camp. Is he one of yours?" Freya asked.

The constable immediately made an odd bird call and received one in return. "That would be one of our rangers."

"Do not kill him, Pohla!" Freya ordered.

Strange, he noted, they should not have noticed that ranger. They were armed and had posted a guard but this still worried him. So far, all he had seen were women and their leader appeared to be this Freya.

"I see only you women. Did something happen to your party while on the road?" he asked.

"Many things happened on the road but, no, we are six women and a halfling, companions traveling together." Freya replied.

"These are perilous times and the roads not often safe. You were lucky to get here."

ORC HAI!

"Thank you for your concern, but we are more than capable of defending ourselves. May I ask who I am addressing?"

"Ah yes. Your pardon, I forget my manners. I am Warrick, senior constable."

"Come on, Warrick. We cannot stay here flirting all night." one of the other riders joked.

Warrick came closer into the light. "I must be off: my comrades grow impatient. But if I can be of any assistance, feel free to look me up." He bowed then turned and started to leave.

"Wait. We have need of a good but not too expensive place to stay and some items that need evaluating?" Freya asked hopefully.

At first Freya thought she had misunderstood his offer as he vaulted onto his horse but then he swung around.

"Try the Doppelganger Inn. Tell Jim I sent you. Once you are settled, come up to the castle and ask for me. I will get you a fair price for your items." With that, he spurred his horse and sped away.

"Oooh! I think he likes you, Freya." Fina cooed good-naturedly.

"Do not be ridiculous. If anything, Aidelle caught his eye." Freya countered. This caused Aidelle to blush but secretly, Freya was a bit flattered.

"Enough of this foolishness. Everyone, come here. I meant to do this in the morning but now is as good a time as any." Freya doled out five more gold and fifty copper pieces to each of them.

"Remember, this is a big town and we will probably be here for a few days looking for work. So, you do not have to buy the first thing you see." Freya advised. "Let's try and get some sleep. We want to be at our best for tomorrow."

"Well, someone needs to be at her best." Fina teased again as Freya walked away and everyone laughed.

The morning meal was skipped as all anticipated a better meal in town. On the road into town, Freya had time to make some more observations. The town itself was protected by an eight-foot high, stone wall. This was not the finely cut uniform stone masonry of the castle. The stones here were of different shapes and sizes. Atop this wall was a six-foot wooden stockade, made of well-fitting upright standing logs all of a uniform size. These had been leveled off across the top then ramparts had been cut in them for the defenders. There was also a series of wooden towers spaced evenly along this wall.

To Freya, they looked like little forts on stilts. Each tower flew a long red and black pendant. In fact, every tower around the town and castle flew a red and black pendant and they were all manned.

It was a big town, bigger than anything she had ever seen, although she could see little of the town itself from outside: only a few buildings were tall enough to be seen over the town walls.

The town wall bulged out from the castle in an elongated circular fashion. The entrance to the town and castle was at its southern end.

There was another impressive gatehouse built in the same fashion as the castle with large finely cut uniform size blocks and rising thirty feet high, housing two large heavy wooden gates reinforced with iron bands.

ORC HA!

A pair of forty-foot, rounded towers were attached one to each side of the gatehouse. Then, for about fifty feet to each side of those towers, the stone and wood palisade had been replaced by finely cut uniform size stones. This was obviously an ongoing project.

About an hour after departing their camp, they reached the gatehouse. It was busy first thing in the morning, especially with arriving and departing caravans, which were given first priority.

Soon enough, it was their turn and they moved forward. Two armored guards carrying poleaxes flanked the gates. They wore red and black checkerboard surcoats over heavy scale armor.

Another pair stood watch just inside the gates, insuring everyone paid their entry tax. A clerk in purple robes sat at a desk collecting and logging down each coin. The fee was one silver piece per head, which the baron used to improve the town walls.

Pre-warned of the figure by Karl, Freya had the seven silvers ready. This seemed to be appreciated, but the only reaction came from the captain of the guard.

"Good lord, ladies! What in the world are you doing out here in the frontier alone?" It was not that he had not seen female warriors before but it was always in a mixed party.

"We thank you for your concern, kind sir. Perhaps you could possibly direct us to the Doppelganger Inn?" Freya asked politely. That seemed to be the right approach.

"The Doppelganger, eh? A good choice but a bit tricky to find on your first time to our fair town. Here, I will take you there myself. It would not be right to leave you to find your way alone."

He took them under his wing and escorted them to the inn. Along the way, he noted points of interest and places to avoid. In this way, they located the guild halls, an armorer and the best shops to buy just about anything you could think of or desire. There were also places he advised them to avoid.

"There you go, ladies. The Doppelganger Inn." He bowed, having safely escorted them to their destination.

"Thank you, captain. My companions and I appreciate your kindness." Freya bowed in appreciation. He then bade them farewell and departed.

A large painted sign identified it as the Doppelganger Inn. It was a well-built two-story whitewashed structure, with a porch in the front and windows on both floors.

"No point standing and gawking out front," Freya suggested. Pohla tied Jack up to a hitching post out front and they moved their gear onto the Inns porch. They could keep an eye on their things while Freya checked them in.

19

Upon entering the inn, they were met and greeted by a young girl with long blonde hair and blue eyes. Freya was not good at guessing age, but thought she was in her mid-teens and guessed she would be the owner's daughter.

"Good morning to you, ladies. My name is Liv. How may I help you?" She curtsied, smiling warmly at them.

Freya noted the first floor of the inn was a tavern, much like the Boar's Head in Anvil, except this one was larger, cleaner and furnished nicer. Obviously, the young girl had been straightening and cleaning up.

"And a good morning to you. Senior constable Warrick recommended your establishment to us. There are seven in our party. I do hope you can accommodate us."

"Oh, yes, we could put you all in the maiden's suite for ten coppers daily. It will be cozy with six, a bit tight with seven. The gentleman should probably have his own room for another six coppers." Liv suggested.

"Yes, that will be fine. We will pay for a week in advance." This brought a smile from Liv and Freya quickly counted out the copper pieces.

"Are you still serving a morning meal?" Tauna asked hopefully.

"Of course!" Liv confirmed scooping up the coins.

"Very good. Let us get settled in then we will be right back down. Oh, we have a donkey tied up out front. Is there a place for him?" Freya asked.

"I will have Ben, the stableboy, retrieve him." Liv then escorted them and their gear up to their rooms. "I will leave you to get settled in. If you need anything else, just call me." As she turned to depart, she added. "Do not worry, Ben will take good care of your donkey."

Being hungry, they quickly deposited their gear and were back down to look for a meal. Liv showed them to a private booth and presented them with something they had never seen before—menus. On it, there were three breakfast meal choices.

First, something called a "Travelers Meal" for one copper piece, consisting of porridge, toast and preserves, tea and buns. Then the "Teamster's Meal" for two copper pieces and consisting of all of the above plus sausage and eggs.

Finally, the "Knight's Meal" for three copper pieces, consisting of all the above with pancakes, honey and mead.

After some confusion and discussion, they all settled for the Teamster's Meal. Freya doled out fourteen copper and they settled in to wait breakfast, which, when it arrived, pleasantly surprised them by how large it was.

They took their time to savor and enjoy this rare luxury. As the meal wound down, Freya spelled out her plans. "We will load my pack up with our treasure, including a couple of those scales. Then we will find out what it is all worth and if

ORC HAI!

we are lucky maybe someone at the castle can identify these scales. Who knows, maybe they are worth selling. I will take some of our money but we will have to find somewhere to hide the rest."

"Freya, the inn will probably have a strongbox for securing valuables." Aidelle pointed out.

"Oh," this caught Freya by surprise, "really? I did not know that. Thank you, Aidelle." She pondered. "Well, if they do, we will place our funds there."

Freya was pleasantly surprised by how much helpful information Aidelle had and was reminded again of just how much of the world of men she and her sisters knew nothing about. They were lucky to have Fordoc and Aidelle. Catching Liv's attention, she signaled her over.

"Yes, ma'am?" Liv asked politely.

"Liv, does the inn have a strongbox for securing clients valuables?" Freya queried.

"Oh, yes ma'am. We have the best. A magical strongbox. It is far more safe and secure than a regular strongbox." Liv boasted proudly.

"That is very good. We have some valuables we would like to put in it but we will have to go back to our room and collect them, then we will be right back down." Freya explained.

"Very good, ma'am. I will tell Jim to expect you." Liv replied.

"Well, that worked out better than I hoped." Freya continued as Liv departed. "We collect everything, deposit our extra money in the strongbox, then it is off to the castle to meet with Warrick." She finished.

"Ooooh, Warrick." Fina cooed nudging Tauna.

"Enough of that, you two." Freya jokingly chastised Fina. Meanwhile, her sister and Tauna exchanged looks.

Once they had finished their meal, they rose from their booth to return to their rooms and, after a bit of sorting, they were back downstairs. Freya decided they should go out with only their broadswords—well, except for Scara, who donned her helmet, for as she put it, "you do not want my ugly mug messing things up." And Pohla, who would not let her prized bow or her throwing knives out of her sight.

Downstairs, in the lobby, the owner Jim was waiting for them. "Good morning, ladies. You have some valuables you wish to lock up?"

"Warrick?" Freya stuttered shocked at seeing him.

He laughed as they all gaped at him. Jim could have been the identical twin of Warrick. "So, Master Warrick sent you here? I understand your confusion. You are not the first. Ever since I arrived here, people have mistaken me for Warrick and believe it or not, I am no relation to him. That is how I came up with the name for this place. Liv tells me you will be staying with us for a few days."

"Yes, at least until we can find work." Freya informed him still a bit bemused.

"There is a lot of work for women here." Jim was sure this was not the kind of work they were looking for but just making conversation.

"Well, we have done enough of that for two lifetimes and are looking for something more rewarding." Freya explained.

He suspected as much but also knew this would be a hard sell to the merchants here. Caravan guard or other such jobs were the domain of men.

ORC HAI!

"I wish you luck. So come on now, let's secure those valuables." His easy-going, good-natured personality shone through in his words. He led them into his back office.

"Liv told us your strongbox is magical?" Freya inquired.

"Is Liv your daughter?" Tauna blurted out curious.

Jim smiled and responded to Tauna's inquiry first. "No, Liv is Warrick's baby sister and yes, my strongbox is magical. This key opens it," he pulled a key on a chain from around his neck.

"I know what you are thinking—what if someone steals the key. It would do them no good, for no one but the property owner can retrieve his or her goods. The secret is that you must, choose a password as you place your valuables inside. It can be as simple as your name. The box will remember and recognize your voice. Only your voice can retrieve your property. It works along the same principle as a bag of holding." Their blank stares alerted him to Freya's next question.

"What is a bag of holding?" Freya asked.

"A bag of holding is a magical bag, larger on the inside than on the outside. It doesn't weigh anything, no matter how full you stuff it. Another really popular feature is that everything stays where you place it." Jim explained.

"They must be terribly expensive?" Freya asked for this really fascinated her.

"Yes. I think they now sell for twenty-five hundred gold pieces, if the guild master likes you."

"Twenty-five—hundred?" Freya stuttered. "Your strongbox must have cost a king's ransom."

"Well, not quite that much but, yes, it would have sold for a fortune except I made it."

They stared at him in disbelief.

"You're a wizard!" Tauna blurted.

"No, but I apprenticed in the Wizards Guild for many years but eventually I found it not for me. So, I packed up my things and left, bringing my nearly completed strongbox with me and came here. I opened this establishment and have never regretted my decision. I completed the strongbox here."

Thoroughly impressed, Freya began to hand over their bags of money.

"No." He reminded her. "You must place them in the strongbox and assign it a password."

Freya thought on this for a moment, then placed the three large bags of coins into the strongbox. "Chimera," was all she said and watched as the bags vanished. There was a collective gasp of astonishment from those crowded around her.

"When you want your possessions back, use your password and they will appear right where you placed them." Jim closed the lid and it locked.

Just then, a thought came to Freya. "What happens if I am killed?"

"In that case, the spell is broken and your possessions will reappear in the strongbox. The baron would then be called in to take possession of them and hold them until your heir or companions arrive to lay claim to them."

That seemed fair enough to Freya.

"The baron does charge for this service, however, and the rates vary by how much you have and if he likes you or not. If no one arrives to lay claim the treasure within a reasonable time, the baron will lay claim to it." Jim finished.

Still, it was better than the alternative of being robbed and losing everything. Then Freya got another idea. "Jim, we acquired a ring and were told it was magical. Can you tell, or is there a way to learn, what kind of magic ring it is?" She asked hopefully. "Someone told us the quickest way was to put it on. Not the safest but quickest. She was sure it was not malevolent. Frankly, we were nervous to try that."

"Yes, that is the quickest but not the safest or the wisest choice. About the best I can do is confirm for you if it is safe to try on. Let me see it."

That was better than nothing. Freya dug into a concealed pouch and pulled out the ring. She carefully handed it to him. Like Varina, Jim had her drop it into his palm. He then carefully examined the ring.

"A moonstone! How unique! This ring is made of Mithral and very old. Probably of elf design. They like moonstones. Oh yes, there is definitely strong magic here." Jim recited an incantation in a language they did not understand. Suddenly, his eyes lit up and he turned to smile at her.

"Your friend was correct; there are no malicious emanations from it. My guess is it is a dual ring of protection of some kind. Sorry I cannot be more specific but it is definitely safe to wear."

"Thank you, thank you so much. You have assisted us far more than we could have hoped." Freya said.

"For a nominal fee, the guild can be more specific. It might be a good idea." Jim suggested.

"We will think on that. Now, however, we have an appointment to meet Warrick at the castle."

"Well, you should stick to the main street. It is the quickest, easiest and safest way." He suggested.

It was good advice for the town off the main street was a maze-like warren of alleys and streets. The majority of reputable shops, guild halls, temples, offices and inns, even the occasional street vendor, occupied the main street. The buildings here were an assortment of one- and two-story structures.

Down the side streets was where you would find the small shops, markets, stables, brothels, taverns and pubs. Here also were the innumerable street vendors, urchins, plus the assorted flotsam and jetsam of everyday life. The buildings here tended towards one-story hovels.

Freya led them out onto the main street, where constables in red livery with black trim moved in pairs through the crowds. At first, they window shopped, but quickly learned that this tended to draw the merchant out, trying to sell them something, so they forged on.

It was not long before the castle gatehouse loomed into view in front of them. The gatehouse was an imposing sight. A full forty feet high and built of the same huge finely cut stones as the keep and fitted together by a master smith.

Archery ports festooned the second through fourth floors while parapets across the top provided protection and more firing positions. Carved boar heads flanked the gates, hiding channels with which to allow the flow of boiling water or oil to rain down on an enemy's head.

The gates themselves were two massive wooden doors reinforced with iron and set back from the walls to allow for a portcullis to drop in front. The gates were currently swung open and the heavy iron portcullis in front of them was raised.

Again, two guards stood out front. They wore red and black checkerboard livery and carried poleaxes, with broadswords at their sides for good measure. Unlike the town guards, they wore heavy chainmail under their livery and banded metal hardened leather helmets like the one Warrick had worn.

Freya marched right up to the guards before she was challenged.

"State your business, miss?" He asked politely but firmly.

These two men were veterans and, while appearing at ease, were ready for any sign of trouble. There were probably archers or crossbowmen aimed at them from any number of archery ports. Not that they were planning to cause any trouble.

"We have come to see senior constable Warrick. He is expecting us." Freya explained politely but firmly.

"Ah yes! You would be the Lady Freya then. Master Warrick did mention you would be along. He is up at the keep, reporting on an incident last night."

"Nothing serious, I hope?" Freya queried.

Fina discreetly nudged Tauna in the ribs, who then gave a nod of understanding.

"Nothing Master Warrick and the constables could not handle, miss, but the baron always wants to hear firsthand of the happenings on his land. I best arrange an escort for you up to the keep. Corporal!" He called out.

There was a hurried trampling of feet and a bearded guard, also in red and black checkerboard livery and similarly armed and armored, appeared.

"Yes, sergeant?"

"Beorn, these young ladies need an escort up to the keep. Master Warrick is expecting them."

Beorn glanced over at them then back to the sergeant. "Sure, Sarge."

"Well, don't just stand there, man!" He then turned to Freya. "Lady Freya, Beorn will take you to the keep." The sergeant gave a slight bow to Freya.

The courtyard beyond the gatehouse was clean and uncluttered. There were barracks, stables and practice fields for archery and combat where, right now, numerous recruits were being put through their paces by drill instructors. The archery field caught Pohla's eye. She had never seen these colorful bull's-eye targets before. Back at Chimera, live targets were most common but when those were not available straw dummies were employed. Beorn noticed her curiosity and that she carried a bow.

"That looks like a nice bow, miss. Are you any good with it? I am a fair archer myself." He queried.

Always shy with strangers, Pohla was hesitant to speak, but Fordoc wasn't. "Better than a halfling with a sling or any man I have yet to see!" He boasted in support of her.

"Now that I would like to see. A challenge it is then." Beorn announced cheerfully before Freya could intercede.

There was nothing Freya could do about it now. This was not at all how she envisioned this trip to the castle. Although everyone so far had been accommodating and friendly, Freya still wished to not draw attention to herself and her sisters.

"Olaf! Be a good lad and get my bow!" Beorn hailed a recruit and a blond-haired boy sprinted off.

This seemed to get everyone's attention and a crowd quickly gathered. Almost as quickly, odds were set and bets placed. All this attention made Pohla and Freya nervous.

A grizzled drill instructor came over as Pohla pulled her bow out of its protective sheath. He whistled in appreciation.

ORC HAI!

"Now that is the finest elf bow, I have ever seen, miss, and I have seen a few."

Pohla smiled meekly at the compliment.

"Beorn is a good shot, miss, but he doesn't stand a chance against this bow," He spoke quietly but reassuringly to her then, much louder, taunted Beorn. "Beorn, I hope you have not wagered too much."

He winked at Pohla then hurried off to place a bet. He was back in less than a minute, offering moral support as Beorn's bow arrived. It was a handsome looking longbow of excellent materials and craftsmanship.

The rules were simple enough. Three targets were set up, each at a different range. Each contestant was to fire one arrow at each, alternating the firing order. Pohla was so nervous she misunderstood the instructions, having never been in a contest of any kind before.

Lots were drawn and Pohla was to fire first. This did nothing to steady her nerves but then the grizzled drill instructor stepped up and gave her some last-minute advice.

"Relax, lass. Focus on the arrow and the target. Let the bow do the rest." It was good advice because it got her mind off the crowd and allowed her to focus on what she always did when she fired her bow.

Stepping up to the mark, she prepared to fire to the cheers of support from her sisters and a big hug from Fordoc. As he stepped away, she raised her bow.

Pohla fired three arrows in rapid succession. There was a collective gasp of stunned astonishment from the collected throng as the three arrows struck their respective targets at the same time. The biased crowd groaned as they could tell Pohla's arrows were all bull's-eyes.

The spotters called in to confirm the bad news for Beorn that, indeed, they were all dead center bulls-eyes. This seemed to stun and deflate the crowd.

Well, with one exception. There was a huge roar of support from the drill instructor. "Way to go, lass! The name is Angus and you have given Beorn something to worry about." He gently patted her on the shoulder in a fatherly fashion.

"Thank you for your support, Angus, I am Pohla."

"Well, mistress Pohla, you can see Beorn is having second thoughts about this contest," he winked at her then shouted another taunt towards Beorn. "So, Beorn, are you ready to admit the lady has beaten you?"

20

Beorn was arguing with the judges about how a rule violation should invalidate the contest when Warrick showed up. He had been with the baron, reporting on the night's events and seen the crowd forming. A quick look and he realized what was going on. Beorn was up to his old tricks: instigating an archery contest to make a profit.

This time, however, it was with those women he had met on patrol last night. He had excused himself and hustled down to intervene but arrived too late to stop it. He was however, in time to see Pohla's three arrows land.

"What is going on here, then?" He looked out towards the targets, noting the arrows placement, then back to Freya and smiled.

"Master Warrick. I was just escorting these women up to the keep to see you and a discussion broke out about archery. Being a fine archer myself, I was just giving them the opportunity to test out the range." Beorn began making excuses, probably hoping Warrick would cancel the contest.

Warrick looked down range again and would have none of it. "Honestly, Beorn, I think she's too good for you."

Perhaps Warrick wounded his pride or he was just worried about losing face so Beorn stepped up to the firing line to a raucous round of cheers. He raised his bow, took careful aim and fired. He repeated the procedure two more times. Compared to the speed with which Pohla delivered her shots, he could have been a crossbowman. All who watched could not help but notice the speed and accuracy difference between the two.

Many were shocked but none could argue what their eyes clearly saw when the spotters awarded the victory to Pohla, as all three of her shots were clearly better. Only two of Beorn's shots nearly matched hers but the third clearly did not.

Freya was surprised Beorn was so gracious in defeat and offered congratulations and a handshake. Pohla was flattered and embarrassed by the win.

Then, out of nowhere, Angus appeared with a couple of bags of coins. "I knew you could do it, lass." He gave her a big hug then presented her with one of the bags. "Your share of our winnings."

"But—no, no, no!" Pohla protested feeling she had not earned it.

Warrick intervened. "Take it, you earned it."

Not knowing what else to do, Pohla accepted the bag with another hug of gratitude.

"So, Angus, you finally managed to get one back on Beorn."

"Aye, Master Warrick, I did at that. Of late, he has gotten overconfident and needed to be taken down a peg. Maybe next time Beorn will pay more attention to an opponent's equipment. Either way this will send him back to the practice field."

ORC HAI!

"How did you know she could beat him?"

"Have you had a good look at the lass's bow, Master Warrick."

"To tell the truth, Angus, in all the excitement I have not had the opportunity."

"Well, Master Warrick, have a good look, a real good look now. I've never seen an elf bow of this quality."

That certainly peaked Warrick's curiosity for he knew Angus had plenty of experience in these matters. "Freya, would—" He paused, realizing he did not know their names as proper introductions had not happened. "We will have to spend some time soon on introductions."

Freya knew what he wanted and interrupted him. "Her name is Pohla and you best ask her permission."

"Of course. You are correct," Warrick turned to Pohla. "Mistress Pohla, your pardon. May I examine your bow?"

Unsure, Pohla looked at Freya and her companions for guidance. It was the encouraging nod from the grizzled veteran Angus that finally convinced her. He reminded her of Odred the chief animal handler at Chimera. She withdrew the bow from its case and handed her prize bow to Warrick.

As he grasped it, the bow gave him a mild shock, startling him and causing him to release his hold on it. Pohla caught it but, to those standing around, it appeared to leap out of his hands and into hers.

"I am sure of it now. That is a high elf bow. That shock you felt was the bow letting you know that you are not its master," Angus announced.

"You might have warned me, Angus!" Warrick demanded a bit harshly, rubbing his hand.

"Sorry, Master Warrick. You best not grasp it again. The next time the shock will be more intense. It should be okay to touch it but let young Pohla hold her bow while we examine it."

"I am so sorry, Warrick." Pohla apologized.

"Not your fault, lass. Few people know that elf weapons can be tricky." Angus assured her.

"I had heard that but was unsure whether to believe it." Freya put in. That was why she had been so scared when Pohla picked up the bow.

"No harm done, Pohla." Warrick assured her. "Not your fault." Warrick was still a little shaken, but his assurance seemed to relax Pohla somewhat.

Warrick suddenly remembered something Freya had said when they first met. "Freya, you were not kidding back at the camp when you told Pohla not to kill the ranger were you?"

"No, I was not kidding. Someone was skulking around our camp. We thought him a bandit or such." Freya admitted.

"You got a bead on one of our rangers last night, lass?" Angus asked Pohla.

"Yes, Fina spotted him for me." Pohla reluctantly admitted.

"She should not have been able to do that." Warrick mused.

"It's the bow, Master Warrick." Angus advised then hugged Pohla to reassure her she had done nothing wrong.

"Shall we try this again?" Warrick asked and Pohla nodded. "Pohla, could you please hold your bow out so I may examine it."

Pohla was happy to oblige and held her bow out so Warrick could run his fingers over it. He noted the workmanship was superb. However, it was Angus who pointed out the finer points.

"No dust settles on it and no marks mar it. Look for any elven script, Master Warrick."

Warrick's fingers passed over the grip and elven script appeared.

"Woe! Look at that!" Angus pronounced. "That, seals it; there is strong elf magic in this bow. Definitely a high elf bow." Everyone seemed surprised, except for Pohla.

"I cannot read high elf and I do not know if the baron can." Warrick admitted.

Even Angus shook his head indicating he did not either.

"It says 'Fly fast, fly true. I can never disappoint you." Pohla informed them.

"Pohla, when did you learn to read elven script?" Freya asked bewildered.

"You know I cannot, Freya." Pohla answered.

"Then how do you know what it says?" Freya was perplexed, and she was not the only one.

"The bow told me. I have known from the first time I touched her." Pohla tried to explain the complicated link she had with her bow.

"More elf magic!" Angus pronounced.

"So, it would appear. Thank you, Pohla." Warrick said.

At a loss for any other explanation, Freya had to agree with their conclusion.

"Well, best be quiet about this or Beorn will cry foul." Warrick whispered. "Not that it will do him any good but perhaps we should continue this up at the keep. I think the baron will wish to meet you." Warrick raised his voice for

Beorn to hear, for he had moved off quite a distance and stood there sulking. "Beorn, I will escort the ladies from here. Return to your duties."

You could tell Beorn was happy to be rid of these women.

Pohla had made forty silver and two gold pieces from her cut of the winnings. A tidy sum but nothing compared to Fordoc's score. From the wager of fifteen gold and fifteen silver pieces, he tripled his return.

The stroll up to the keep was mixed with introductions and casual talk. Ahead of them loomed the four-story castle keep. It was roughly rectangular in shape with rounded towers at all corners and obviously built by a master craftsman using finely cut stone blocks.

Built with defense in mind, arrow slits had been carefully placed strategically around the walls while the towers had been incorporated into each corner.

A broad, stone staircase led up to a wooden drawbridge and the second floor

Entrance, where stood two guardsmen dressed in red and black livery. These men carried crossbows and wore broadswords at their sides. They stood in front of two open heavy wooden doors, wrapped with bands of iron.

Freya and her party climbed the stairs and crossed the drawbridge. It was here that Freya noticed another heavy iron portcullis, which could also be lowered to further deter an attacker. The guards smartly saluted Warrick and let them pass unchallenged.

The first floor of the keep housed storerooms, the kitchen and servants' quarters. The majority of the second floor was taken up with the Great Hall, where formal banquets were held. Above this was the third floor, which housed offices, more storerooms and limited living quarters.

Then there was the fourth floor. This was the baron's floor, consisting of a private meeting and dining hall along with living quarters for his family.

Upon reaching the second floor, Warrick led them over to a set of spiral stairs. It was on the way to the staircase that Tauna got to the heart of a curious point she wished clarified.

"Warrick?" she began.

"Yes, Tauna."

"Why does everyone call you, Master Warrick?"

He gave a jovial laugh. "For generations now, my family has served the barons as their stewards here at Haghill. For all intents and purposes, that means we run the household: thus, the title Master of the Household. Master for short."

"So, you are nobility?" Freya asked just to clarify the correct etiquette so as not to offend. "Should we be calling you Master Warrick, too?"

"In a way yes, but do not hold that against me," He joked. "But I would prefer it if you just called me Warrick."

As Warrick led them up the spiral staircase toward the fourth floor. Scara took note of the stairs' strategic position.

"Warrick, these stairs seem to favor a defender. Was that by design?" She queried.

"Yes, Scara, they were deliberately designed with that mind."

Emerging onto the fourth floor, the first thing they noticed was a pair of large ornate wooden doors. Warrick stepped up to them and rapped on them with his knuckles. Shortly thereafter, a panel slid open and a wrinkled old face appeared.

"Ah, young Master Warrick," He identified Warrick then turned. "Young Master Warrick with company, Your Lordship," he announced.

"Fine, Jeeves. Show them in." a deep voice replied from somewhere farther back in the room.

The door swung open to allow them entrance. Freya noted this, too, was a heavy door and not easily broken down, for this was the baron's private hall. A smaller and fancier version of the second floor's Great Hall; however, this hall had a vaulted ceiling supported by carved stone pillars, which rose up then curved out into multiple arms while wooden beams branched off from each arm to form a network of beams supporting the ceiling and giving it a very cathedral like appearance.

Here, in this private sanctum, fewer banners hung from the rafters replaced by more ornate tapestries. There were also fewer tables and, at the far end on a raised dais, sat a simple but comfortable looking chair. Currently however the baron was seated at a table.

Baron Hagar rose as they entered. He was a big burly fellow with short dark curly hair, lightly speckled with gray, bushy eyebrows, blue eyes and a well-trimmed beard, which outlined a handsome face. Around his shoulders was draped a dark fur trimmed cloak.

Baron Hagar immediately realized what an odd group this was and understood why they had fascinated his young steward.

One for sure was part orc and perhaps the pretty archer was part elf. All but one of this unique collection of women was of mixed blood. But what was a halfling doing amongst them. All these thoughts rolled through his head as they approached.

ORC HAI!

Warrick took the lead and stepped forward to greet his liege. He bowed and Freya, her sisters and Fordoc followed his example. Warrick had prepared them as best he could for what was expected of them.

"Baron Hagar, here are the travelers I was telling you about," Warrick addressed the baron then began introductions. "This is Freya their leader."

"Normally I would have welcomed you to the frontier but from what Warrick has told me—you are already well acquainted with it. So let me just welcome you to Haghill."

"Thank you, Your Lordship. You have a fine city here." Freya replied with a bow.

"City," he began with a laugh. "My word, Lady Freya, just how far north, are you from? Haghill is just a respectable sized barony. The real city is to the south. Edradour it is called."

"But I thought, after seeing Anvil." She tried to explain.

"Anvil! Good lord, that barely qualifies as a town." He joked.

Freya was at a loss. "But Haghill seems so big and bustling compared to Anvil or anything we have seen so far."

"Being on the frontier, I suppose we do look quite stately." Warrick added seeing her confusion.

"Yes, I suppose you are right, Warrick. Now show me the vixen who bewitched my best archer!" The baron commanded.

Pohla did not realize he was joking. She immediately turned beet red, forgot all protocols and began apologizing as tears began to flow.

A woman, who had been observing quietly in the wings, rushed over, sweeping Pohla up in her arms. "Men!" she hmphed.

Freya noted her bearing was that of nobility and she was very attractive, with fair skin, blue eyes and long wavy blonde hair held in place by a simple gold hairband. She wore a long, silky, pale blue dress that looked expensive and she was probably only a few years younger than the baron.

"You must pardon my husband's poor taste in words and humor. He often forgets his manners!" she gave him a disapproving look.

"Fiona!" Hagar blustered.

"Yes, My Lord," She replied sweetly, then continued to console Pohla. "There, there, little one. So, you are the one who finally bruised Beorn's inflated ego. Good for you! Do not let my husband's bluster upset you. He was just as happy to see it happen. My husband may come across as a gruff old bear—" she carefully dabbed away at Pohla's tears with a handkerchief. "But he is really a kind, loving, gentle soul whom I am lucky to have." She finished with a brilliant smile for him. There followed an awkward moment of silence.

"Hrrmph," Jeeves cleared his throat. "Perhaps we should continue the introductions."

With that timely intervention of Jeeves, the rest of the introductions went off flawlessly.

Warrick waited patiently but he very much wished the baron to see Pohla's bow before the meeting was over.

"My Lord, you should have a look at mistress Pohla's bow. It is very special."

"Well, if you think it necessary. Pohla, my dear, may I see your bow?" The baron asked politely and put his hand out.

"Of course, my Lord," She began to take her prized bow out and suddenly remembered the shock her bow gave

ORC HAI!

Warrick. "Well," She hesitated, "you may touch it, my Lord, but not hold it." She apologized tactfully.

"Oh yes! She is quite correct. Angus got me to try to hold it and the bow gave me quite a shock when I did." Warrick explained.

The baron immediately withdrew his hand. "Anything else you have forgotten to tell me, Warrick?"

"High elven script in the handle," He sheepishly admitted.

"So, it is a high elf bow?"

"That was Angus's opinion."

"Well, he should know. Pohla, could you show me the script please?"

"Of course, my Lord," And Pohla held out the bow for him to examine and ran her finger over the grip and the fancy swirling style of elven script appeared.

"Fly fast, fly true, I can never disappoint you." Both Hagar and Pohla repeated.

"You hear her too?" Pohla asked happily.

"Sadly, no, but I can read high elven script, Pohla."

"Oh." She seemed disappointed.

The baron leaned in close and whispered in her ear. "She will only answer to you. Do not be sad, for you are truly blessed to have her. You must have some elf in you: it is the only way the bow would bond to you." He then gave her a gentle fatherly hug.

Before leaving, Freya and her companions received an invitation to return and dine with Baron Hagar and Lady Fiona in his private hall at the keep. It was when Warrick escorted them down a floor to have their treasure evaluated that Aidelle pointed out what she foresaw as a problem.

"Freya, what are we going to wear?"

"Not to worry." Warrick said. "I know just the shop to find something appropriate."

A moment later and they found themselves at an office on the third floor. "Tobias, this is Lady Freya and her companions. She has some treasure for you to evaluate." Warrick introduced them to a scholarly looking old gentleman dressed in dark purple robes. A long heavy gold chain with a scale pendant hung around his neck.

As Freya laid out their treasure on his desk, he studied each piece carefully.

"Well, Tobias? What do you think?" Warrick asked.

"Hmmm. These five gemstones are zircons, worth fifty gold apiece. The gold cup another fifty, the silverware another forty."

So, Freya thought, the appraisals she got from Karl were accurate. Not that she expected anything else.

Tobias sorted through the other gemstones. "These two are tiger's eyes, worth only ten gold each. Here is a bloodstone worth, say fifty gold. Now these are nice," he held up the jade, the red coral and the peridot. "Worth five-hundred gold apiece."

Freya eyes began to widen in surprise.

"I held the best for last. These two are blue topaz," Tobias indicated the gems in question. "One thousand gold for each of them. A pity you do not have more of them. Now I make the total tally to be three-thousand-nine-hundred-ten gold pieces."

ORC HAI!

Freya hardly knew what to say. The appraisal was far higher than her wildest expectation. Meanwhile, Tobias began placing bags of coins on the desk.

Each bag was sealed with wax and carried a denomination denoting the value contained within it, five hundred being the largest.

Freya finally managed to regain her voice. "Thank you very much, Tobias." She carefully picked up each bag and placed them in her pack.

"A pleasure, Lady Freya," Tobias replied sliding the extra ten gold pieces to her, thinking how seldom he had served anyone so amiable. People were always squabbling over his evaluations.

"Thank you again, Tobias." Freya bowed to him before leaving.

"So where are we off to now?" Warrick inquired.

"Well, if it is not too much trouble, the Wizard's Guild. We have some potions and a ring that needs identifying. Oh, and we need to find out what these are and if they are valuable?" Freya produced one of the scales.

Warrick's eyes lit up, for he knew immediately what it was. "Oh, ho! Now that is a dragon scale from the chest or belly of the worm." He took the scale from her and examined it more carefully.

"Probably from a big red or a black. If you had a number of them, it would be worth turning into armor. It is pliable like leather but tougher than iron."

This was not something she had contemplated. They now had plenty of money, even if she purchased a bag of holding. Ever since she had been told of them, the thought of owning one intrigued her and now, unexpectedly, they had the money and a lot more. Enough, she suspected, to get custom made armor. Freya's thoughts were suddenly interrupted by Warrick.

"Where did you get these?" he asked. "And why did you not ask Jim to identify this stuff?"

"Why did you not warn us he was your twin and a magic user?" Scara piped up.

"Oops! Yeah, sorry about that but, seriously, where did you get this?" He held up the scale.

"Is it important?" Freya responded still a little distracted by the thought of incorporating them in custom armor.

"Yes. The possibility of a dragon is always important."

"Three days' march back up the road. We spent a couple of nights in a barn by a ruined coach house. Well, that is what Aidelle called it anyway. We cleaned out a large pack of orcs that had been camped there. While searching the area, Aidelle found ten of these."

Freya could see him doing some rapid calculations. "That would have been Rourke's Station. I had almost forgotten about it. It was a real nice place, I was told. They had planned on building another one farther north, about two thirds of the way to Anvil. Then, one day it was gone. No one survived to tell the tale. So now we know a dragon was responsible."

"And some orcs finished off the remains." Scara added.

"That would have been a lot later. Dragons are known to hang around their handiwork and orcs are stupid but not that stupid." Warrick clarified. He then paused, mulling over reports in his head.

ORC HAI!

"So where did the worm go? There have been no reported sightings of a dragon. I will have to tell the baron of this but, as the dragon has moved on, there is no hurry."

By this time, they exited the keep and began to make their way across the grounds of the outer bailey. Pohla waved to Angus, who was back putting recruits through their paces, but not too busy to respond in kind.

"You have made a friend there, Pohla." Warrick teased.

To no one's surprise, there was no sign of Beorn. Even at the gatehouse he was visibly absent.

"I hope we have not made an enemy?" Freya queried Warrick.

"That would be most unwise of him, and Beorn, if nothing else, is a smart man. You may have bruised his ego but nothing could crush it. I bet the next time you meet, there will be no animosity. Trust me. On that note, you never told me why you did not ask Jim about the ring or potions. You saw his magic strongbox, I assume?"

"Oh, yes, it was amazing. And we did ask about the ring. He told us it was made of Mithral and very old, some kind of dual ring of protection and suggested we ask at the Guild for a more accurate appraisal. The potions just slipped my mind for we were in a hurry to get to the castle." Freya explained.

"Mithral? Now that is unusual. Only dwarven miners have been able to unearth it these days. The elves treasure it more than gold and buy up almost all of it. Shines like highly polished silver, is stronger and lighter than iron not to mention it never blackens or rusts." Warrick explained.

"Thank you, Warrick, I was just about to ask you about Mithral." Freya admitted.

"It is a rare material. I am surprised you have not heard of it before."

"We have had no real contact with dwarves or elves." Freya stated.

"You are a real enigma, Freya." Warrick shook his head.

"A good enigma, I hope?"

"Of course!" He replied with a smile.

21

A little later, at the guild hall, they were greeted upon entering by a tall kindly looking gentleman with startlingly blue eyes and sporting a long black beard streaked with gray. He wore dark blue robes trimmed with gold. Emblazoned across the front of his flowing robes were crossed lightning bolts.

"Good day to you, Master Warrick. I see you bring guests to my hall," he was obviously focused on the most important member of the party, Warrick. "The baron's order is not quite finished yet."

"That is fine, Godric. Today I bring you customers. These young ladies are friends and have a ring and some potions that need evaluating."

Godric turned those startling blue eyes on Freya. "There is a fee of five gold pieces per item to evaluate treasure, young mistress."

"Oh, that is fine," Freya stammered under his piercing gaze. "But, please, call me Freya."

"As you wish, Lady Freya. Please call me Godric. A pleasure to meet you."

Freya was not used to being called a lady, but gave in, realizing she could not change things. She began pulling out the potion flasks.

Godric produced a table and had her place them there. She held the ring back for now. To Freya and the untrained eye, the flasks looked all the same. To Godric, one glance and they told him everything he needed to know.

What appeared to the untrained eye to be mere decorations, to those trained like him, these were runes identifying the mixture and mixer. So as long as the seal was intact, the contents should be as marked, but Godric liked to be thorough. Sliding two flasks to the side, he broke the seals and gave them a sniff.

"Healing potion, double healing potion," He pronounced and magically resealed them.

Godric then carefully examined the remaining three. Their seals proved to be intact also, though he broke them open to be sure. To the unenlightened, this probably looked rather mystical and perhaps that was the intent.

One at a time, Godric announced what they were: a potion; of giant strength, a potion: of Invulnerability, a potion: of speed. He then resealed them. Freya marked them with ribbons to help her identify each.

Godric now stood looking expectantly at her. Freya carefully removed the ring from its pouch and placed it on the table. She had learned her lesson. Godric made no attempt to take it or pick it up.

Instead, he quietly uttered some incantation as he passed his hand over it much like Jim had done. Obviously satisfied, he carefully picked it up to examine it further.

ORC HAI!

"This is a very old and rare ring of elf manufacture. Where in the world did you get it?" Godric asked.

"In the mountains many days to the north." Freya offered.

"Probably belonged to a ranger then." Godric announced and Freya quickly looked at Warrick worried.

"Not one of ours." He admitted.

"This is a dual magic ring. It is a ring of protection and will also protect the wearer against charm spells. The ring will adjust its size to fit the wearer. A very nice find." He handed the ring back to her. "Will there be anything else, Lady Freya?"

"Well, I have recently heard of something called a bag of holding. Do you have such a thing and what do they cost?"

"A bag of holding," Godric paused in thought. "Well, Lady Freya, we could have one ready for you in two days for a cost of two-thousand-five-hundred gold pieces."

"Thank you, Godric. Will you pardon me a moment to discuss this with my companions, please."

"Of course, my Lady." Godric stepped away to give them some privacy.

"Well? What do you think?" Freya asked. What she received was puzzled stares.

It was Scara who piped up first saying what they all felt. "Freya, if you think we need it, then buy it. We trust your decision."

The others' nods of agreement were all Freya needed.

"We trust you! You know that!" Scara finished.

Meanwhile, Warrick was in conversation with Godric, probably discussing the baron's order. Whatever that might be. Freya managed to get Warrick's attention and he alerted Godric: a decision had been reached.

"Yes, Lady Freya?" Godric asked as he approached.

"Thank you for being so patient." Freya apologized.

"It is no trouble at all, Lady Freya. So, you have reached a decision?"

"Yes, Godric. I have decided we will purchase that bag of holding. Is there a deposit required?"

Warrick nearly burst into laughter. They all looked at him while Freya gave him a reproving glare.

"Sorry, my apologies, Freya. I keep forgetting your inexperience in so many things Freya. You all show capabilities far beyond your years in other ways.

"Generally, the Guild requires no deposit but let's just say that, of all the shops and guilds, the Wizard's Guild takes an agreement very seriously. The Guild will track down the offender to make them honor their commitment. Not that you would."

Freya appreciated this information and it presented her with an opportunity to prove their good intention.

"Ah, I see. Well, we are new to these parts and therefore an unknown commodity. In light of that, we shall pay up front." With that Freya began fishing out money.

Godric smiled at her intentions. "Lady Freya, that is not necessary as Master Warrick has vouched for you."

"Why thank you, Godric. You are most kind, but I think we will still pay up front."

"As you wish, Lady Freya. And, as you are making a major purchase, the Guild will waive the evaluation fees."

"Thank you, Godric. Now, that reminds me—where can I sell off unwanted potions?"

"I will give you a fair price for any you wish to exchange or sell."

"Oh, excellent! We will be keeping the healing potions but I am unsure of the others and need to think on them."

"I understand, Lady Freya, and I hope we will be able to do business again." He gave her a slight bow, which she returned. With their business settled, they departed.

Their next stop was the Armorer's Hall, where Freya was greeted upon entering by Lars, the owner. Lars was a tall, muscular fellow with blond hair and blue eyes that highlighted his strong handsome features.

Freya displayed her dragon scales and explained what she desired. Lars listened intently while examining one of the scales, then explained just what he would do and the price per set.

His enthusiasm convinced Freya she had the right man for the job, so she commissioned five sets of chain and dragon scale armor, similar to partial plate only lighter because the dragon scale formed the chest and back plates.

She commissioned a sixth set, to look the exactly like the rest only using hardened leather instead of dragon scale with the chainmail. As the armor had to be fitted to the wearer, Scara insisted Aidelle get one of the sets of dragon scale as she would need it more than her.

Afterall, Scara reasoned, Aidelle had found the dragon scales in the first place and, as she was the best swordswoman in the group, she would take the hardened leather set. Freya was not going to argue the point because she believed Aidelle needed the armor more than any of her other sisters.

To go with the new armor, Freya commissioned new cloth hauberks of better quality for under their armor plus new matching iron greaves and vambraces for them all. She also selected four new broadswords and nearly identical scabbards.

Finding armor for Fordoc was more challenging as chainmail was too heavy and he refused to wear exposed armor like the others. In the end, Freya had him fitted for cloth armor—not ideal for protection but he at least could wear it under his clothes.

She did, however, have an idea how to boost his chances. Originally, she had considered loaning the magic ring to Aidelle but perhaps Fordoc would need it more. At least until they could find something better.

Lars advised them that the armor would take a few days to complete. Next, it was on to their chore of purchasing proper evening attire for dinner. Surprisingly enough, that created the most controversy. More surprising was the fact that it was not because of Scara. In fact, she was the least argumentative.

The controversy occurred when Scara selected a racy, red gown with a plunging *V* neckline exposing plenty of her ample bosom. There were even slits in each side running from mid-thigh to the bottom hem and exposing plenty of leg.

Never one to draw attention to herself, Pohla was scandalized at Scara's choice of attire. In contrast, she selected a nondescript, medium green gown in a most conservative style, while Fordoc found a boy-sized tunic and cape.

The others stuck to the more traditional fashion as recommended by the shop owner, Miss Iliana.

Miss Iliana was a plump, jovial, middle-aged woman with a quick wit and the ability to size up a customer and know

ORC HAI!

their mind better than they did. She matched that with what suited them.

All the gowns were made of satin and were sleeveless, with low open collars. While snug fitting to the hips, they opened up at the bottom to flow down, stopping just above the ankle.

Aidelle found a shade of gold to her liking, while Fina chose a rich purple. Tauna surprised them all when she selected black, and Freya liked the purple Fina had chosen but selected a baby blue.

The real fuss started when Scara asked Tauna about an alteration to the fit of her gown and Pohla voiced her displeasure. "You already look like a harlot in that dress! How much more do you want to expose? All anybody is going to see is your boobs hanging out."

"Good. That is what I was going for. At least that way they will not be looking at my ugly mug!" Scara taunted right back.

There was a sudden burst of laughter from everyone except Pohla. Freya, too, was a little concerned about the appropriateness of Scara's gown, but she would not mention it.

"Well, I am not walking through town with her dressed like that," Pohla stated. "What do you think, Warrick? Is that appropriate?"

Caught off-guard and not really wanting to be involved in this, Warrick stalled for time. He realized he would need to be careful with what he said. Pausing in thought, he began to look them over, one by one, pausing on Freya before a final appraisal of Scara and the gown in question.

He got her to do a pirouette for a full inspection. Surprisingly, he liked the effect. "I was not sure at first but the overall effect looks good on you, Scara, and I am pretty sure the baron's sons will like it."

This did not appease Pohla at all. "Men!" She huffed. "I do not care. I am still not walking through town with her dressed like that."

"It was to be a surprise but the baron is sending round a coach to pick you all up. He does not expect his guests to find their own way to his table," Warrick countered, seeing a way to defuse the situation. This seemed to mollify, or at least nullify Pohla's protests.

"My apologizes, ladies, but now I must return to my duties. Lady Freya, if you and your companions are all done, I will help you carry all your beautiful gowns back to the Doppelganger."

Warrick escorted them to the inn and bade them farewell. "I will see you all later." He then bowed to Freya and was off.

Once comfortably settled into their room, Freya proposed her idea for the magic ring. "I think Fordoc should get the ring. He is the smallest and lightest armored of us all."

This was an unfortunate choice of words by Freya and elicited an immediate protest from Scara. "The ring is treasure and it was acquired before Fordoc joined us. If anyone should take the ring Freya, it should be you."

Whether this was a leftover reaction to Fordoc's earlier faux-pas suggestion of using Aidelle for bait or her real belief that Freya, as leader, deserved to reap the benefits of the ring, Freya did not know. It did not matter either way; she would have to defuse her faux pas.

"The ring will still belong to the group. I only meant to loan the ring to him until we can find some better protection for him. I will still keep possession of the ring." Freya clarified and this proved acceptable to Scara.

"Now I propose we keep the healing potions but I see no need to keep the others. Acquiring more healing potions make more sense." Freya offered in an attempt to distract Scara and her sisters. The tactic worked and all agreed they should sell or trade the other potions.

The next order of business was brought up by Tauna who queried about lunch, which elicited a thunder of laughter and lightened the otherwise serious mood.

"Yes, perhaps a late lunch is in order, at least to stave off hunger until dinner. We can see what the inn has to offer or we can venture out and see what else we can find!" Freya proposed.

"If it is all the same to you, I would prefer to venture out after my meal." Scara stated.

"I second the motion!" Tauna piped up.

With no dissenters, they headed downstairs to sample the lunchtime fare. The meals offered were simple yet delicious and filling. After years of slavery and abuse, the sisters felt rather pampered. It was a good feeling but an unfamiliar one and one they all agreed they could easily get used to.

After lunch, it was out to do a little exploring of the town, both to search for work and see what interesting wares this town could provide. The search proved enlightening and, although no acceptable job opportunities presented themselves, there were plenty of interesting and useful items available.

Time passed so rapidly that, before they knew it, it was time to return to the Doppelganger to dress and prepare for dinner with the Lord and Lady of Haghill.

A splendid red and black coach with golden boar heads emblazoned on the side doors arrived to pick them up within the hour. The coach had four spoked wheels and was led by two big black horses. It had a roof to keep out the weather and there were drapes for privacy. Seated in front were a driver and guard plus a coachman on the back. All wore fancy red and black livery.

As Freya and her companions emerged from the inn, the coachman dismounted to offer them assistance. All the sisters wore a long, fancy cape over their gowns to protect them from the cold. Unused to long fancy gowns boarding the coach was a challenging experience although not as much for Scara the slits in her dress proved most useful. It was a big step up into the coach but the coachman knew what he was doing and everyone boarded without a hitch.

Freya had never ridden in a coach like this before, or any kind of coach before, so this was a real treat. Each of them was excited and a bit nervous to dine with the baron and Lady Fiona.

Warrick was there to meet them at the keep's second floor entrance and escort them to the baron's private hall on the fourth floor. He was even more handsome in his dress robes. Taking Freya by the arm, he escorted them up to the baron's hall.

This was to be a more private dinner. They were met and greeted by Baron Hagar and Lady Fiona. What followed was the introduction to their children. Well, all but their eldest son, Haglyn, who was out leading a night patrol in much the same way Warrick had the previous night.

The baron and Lady Fiona had three pretty, blonde daughters: Serafina, Gabrielle and Linayia. All resembled their mother. The eldest, Serafina, was probably close in age to Freya but younger than Warrick. The two younger sons present were Malcolm and Hanwin: twins younger than Gabrielle but older than Linayia.

The evening turned into a splendid affair in which Warrick lavished most of his attention on Freya, much to the obvious dismay of Serafina.

It was apparent to Freya and her sisters that Serafina had feelings for Warrick. She had obviously dressed up especially for him and expected him to notice her, which he did, but Serafina clearly expected more. Something more like the attention he was paying Freya. Freya began to wonder if that was intentional—was he just trying to get a rise out of Serafina?

Freya had no illusions about how far this could go. Warrick was nobility and she was a half-breed mongrel and an ex-slave. Still, she relished the attention he showed her, at least for tonight.

The true challenge came with dinner. The meal was bigger, fancier and better than anything they had ever seen. No meal they had ever served at Chimera compared to this, but that was not the problem. It was proper table etiquette that confused them, for there was none of that in Chimera.

Scara was fortunate for Aidelle quietly and surreptitiously showed her the correct etiquette, while Pohla had Fordoc to guide her through. Alas, Freya, Fina and Tauna struggled, relying on cues from Warrick.

Servants flitted in and out with more food, wine and mead and much of the table conversation revolved around the sisters' adventures up north. Freya was beginning to get good at telling an abridged version of their tale. Everyone was interested in the details, none more than Baron Hagar and Warrick, who were obviously gathering intelligence and a feel for what was going on up north.

When the evening finally came to a close, the same coach and coachman that brought them, waited to take them back to the Doppelganger Inn. Everyone was so exhilarated by the evening's activities that it took them all quite some time to wind down enough to get to sleep. They talked about the attention a certain handsome gentleman lavished on one of their number.

22

It was a late rising for the sisters the next day and, after a hearty breakfast, they ventured out. The Wizard's Guild was their first destination. Freya traded her unwanted potions for three regular healing potions and three extra strength healing potions.

Next, they browsed the shops around town. Freya purchased some more crossbow bolts, inquired about the availability of elven arrows and then, on the advice of Warrick, purchased some holy water and holy symbols—in case they should encounter the undead. All the while, she inquired about caravans needing guards.

By the end of the day, no opportunities had presented themselves but this did not worry Freya. She did start to worry by the end of the third: it was becoming apparent that women were not expected to be or wanted as guards.

Here in Haghill, it seemed women were expected to perform more menial tasks, which Freya had no intention of ever doing again. It may be that the treatment on these jobs would be far superior, pleasant in fact, compared to those experienced in Chimera but adventure was in her blood now and it was all she wanted.

They met Warrick the following day. He came by the Doppelganger Inn to check on how they were getting on. Freya took the opportunity to pick his brain on why they were having such trouble finding employment, even though she already had a good idea. She had decided that, if they did not find something soon, she would lead her sisters south towards that big city in search of opportunities.

"Warrick, everyone has been polite enough but no one will hire us. Oh, we have had plenty of offers for domestic work but, frankly, I would rather cut my own throat than accept them." Freya blushed. "I even used your name to no avail. I hope I did not overstep?"

"No, of course not." He paused, looking at her seriously. "The merchants are a bit cautious here in Haghill. You and your companions are an unknown and unproven commodity. It will take time to break down those opinions."

"I understand. You mean, because we are women." His expression told her this was true. "Well, we are used to far worse treatment. I just wish Karl would return. I think I could talk him into taking us on."

"Karl?" Warrick asked.

"The guard captain on that caravan we rescued. I told you about that, remember?"

"Oh yes, the caravan you rescued from the hobgoblins."

"Yes. I guess we will keep looking for a couple more days. If by then we have found nothing. I think we will go south and have a look at that big city you mentioned."

ORC HAI!

"Big cities have a danger all their own, Freya, so be wary. Stick together and trust no one who tries too quickly to befriend you."

"I will remember that and, who knows, perhaps we will yet find a caravan and cargo in need of a good escort. Either way, we will be back this way. I am sure we will see you before we depart. Of course, I suspect Serafina will be glad to see us away."

Warrick laughed. "You and your sisters are refreshing. You speak your mind. But," here he paused and turned serious again. "Serafina is the baron's eldest daughter and must learn that what she wants is not necessarily what is in her future. I don't know her father's plans for her, but they do not include me."

This startled Freya. "She is not free to choose?" Freya was aghast at this revelation. She was able to stop herself before saying anything she might regret.

"You must understand; for nobility, freedom is a relative term. Often, we have more obligations to family and state that often requires a certain loss of personal choice."

Freya realized she had touched on a sensitive subject. Contrary to his earlier behavior toward Serafina, he did have feelings for her, strong feelings. With this realization, she quickly tried to change the subject.

"We must seem like such simpletons," Freya joked.

"Hardly," he laughed. "So, what are your plans for the day?"

"We planned to go check on our new armor."

"I imagine Lars will have done a splendid job as usual on them."

"I should hope so. He took enough measurements. I thought I was being groped," Scara butted in.

This elicited a hearty laugh all round as they headed off to the armorer to check on their new armor.

"We are having no luck finding elven arrows. Have you any advice?" Freya asked.

"Elven arrows will be tricky," Warrick said. "You may have more luck in Edradour, but even there you will find few, if any. I have some spare time right now. What say we go have a look?"

They arrived and Lars greeted them and hustled them into the back. There hung six virtually identical sets of armor gleaming shiny black with an odd reddish hue around the edges of the breast and back plates. Even the chainmail and scale skirts shined black. How the smith accomplished this eluded Freya.

"I hope they please you, Lady Freya?" Lars inquired as she gaped at his workmanship.

"Wheew!" Warrick whistled. "You have outdone yourself, Lars!" He examined the workmanship.

Lars smiled, pleased, but awaited the approval of Lady Freya.

"Yes! Yes! They are magnificent! I am stunned! You are indeed the master of all Master Craftsman!"

"I am pleased they meet your approval, Lady Freya." Lars bowed to her.

He then insisted they try on each set of armor to ensure a proper fit. This would allow him the opportunity for any final adjustments. The effort proved totally unnecessary as he had

ORC HAI!

done such a superb job and no adjustments were required. Each set fit the owner like a glove.

It was while observing how professional these identical sets of armor made them look that Freya came up with the idea of matching helmets. She would discuss this with her sisters later.

Freya and her sisters were so pleased with their new armor they decided to wear it back to the inn.

Along the way, Freya stopped to inquire about caravans needing guards. Unfortunately, even with the new armor and Warrick present, they received no offers. Frustrated, Freya was considering just joining a caravan heading south as travelers, or working for nothing just to get a foot in the door.

Once again, she thought of Karl the caravan guard captain. It was too bad he had not returned. She was positive he would take them on or, at the very least, vouch for them.

Over dinner that evening, the sisters agreed to commission six new helmets in the same black red as their armor. Freya proposed her idea that, if no job opportunities presented themselves within a day or two, they would head south with the first caravan as travelers. Her idea was well received.

The next morning, on the way to commission those helmets, Fordoc came running over to Freya full of excitement.

"I have found us a job!" He trumpeted. The sisters swarmed around him, wanting to know all the details.

"Tell me about it!" Freya demanded, quieting the clamor.

"I ran into a group of halflings from home in the market selling pipe-weed at a stall. You can hardly imagine my surprise. We struck up a conversation and it turns out they are looking for a group of reasonably-priced guards to escort their cargo of pipe-weed south to Edradour to sell. And then an escort back home to their settlement of Cornerbrook with another cargo. I did not ask what it would be but I did not think it mattered." Pohla gave him a huge hug while the others patted him on the back.

Freya breathed a sigh of relief. "This is good news, Fordoc. When do they wish to depart?"

"They would like to depart tomorrow morning as their business here has concluded."

"That could work for us. I will need to meet with them, but first we will commission our new helmets. I am sure we can agree upon a fee."

At the Armorer's Hall, Lars surprised Freya. Unbeknownst to her, he had prepared six iron Barbute style helmets in the same colors as their armor, in anticipation that they would require them.

So, when Freya inquired about matching helmets, he simply went into the back and reemerged with the six of them, much to her astonishment and delight. All that was needed was any personal alterations, anything from the selection of an alternate trim color to a colored horsehair plume. These minor alterations Lars promised would be ready before the end of the day. As they left, all they could say to each other was how did he know?

Later, Freya met with the group of five pipe-weed merchants from Fordoc's homeland of Cornerbrook. Both groups sized each other up before haggling over a deal.

In reality, Freya had no intention of missing this work opportunity. She would have worked for free and very nearly did, so an agreement was easily reached. Freya would get a food stipend to buy rations for her companions. The halflings would arrange their own meals. Pay would be minimal but all acquired treasure would belong to Freya and her companions.

It was agreed that they would depart early the next day. Freya expected foraging to be more difficult if not impossible on this trip.

Warrick explained that the journey should take three perhaps four days, so Freya had Tauna purchase rations accordingly. Her employers covered the cost with barely a quibble.

THE END

Don't miss the continuing adventures
of Freya and her sisters, in

BOOK TWO: The Trouble with Halflings

About the Author

Thomas Fulton began as an avid gamer many years ago when Dungeons and Dragons was a simple three book set and a lot of imagination. Before the Player's Handbook, Monster Manual and a series of Adventure modules.

When he first began writing this series for fun and loosely based on his gaming adventures he stuck to what he knew and enjoyed while trying to keep it light-hearted and hopes you will enjoy his ramblings.

Thomas lives in Maple Ridge, British Columbia, with his very patient wife. They travel extensively and being huge Tolkien fans have been to New Zealand multiple times.

Printed in Canada